Georgia Hill writes romcoms  published by One More Cha of HarperCollins.

She divides her time between the beautiful counties of Herefordshire and Devon and lives with her two beloved spaniels, a husband (also beloved) and a ghost called Zoe. She loves Jane Austen, eats far too much Belgian chocolate and has a passion for *Strictly Come Dancing*.

www.georgiahill.co.uk

 twitter.com/georgiawrites
 facebook.com/georgiahillauthor

## Also by Georgia Hill

The Little Book Café Series

*The Little Book Café: Tash's Story*

*The Little Book Café: Emma's Story*

*The Little Book Café: Amy's Story*

(Also available together in a bind-up edition)

The Millie Vanilla's Cupcake Café Series

*Spring Beginnings*

*Summer Loves*

*Christmas Weddings*

(Also available together in a bind-up edition)

The Say it with Sequins Series

*The Rumba*

*The Waltz*

*The Charleston*

(Also available together in a bind-up edition)

Standalones

*While I Was Waiting*

# THE GREAT SUMMER STREET PARTY PART 1

## Sunshine and Cider Cake

### GEORGIA HILL

One More Chapter
a division of HarperCollins*Publishers*
1 London Bridge Street
London SE1 9GF
www.harpercollins.co.uk
HarperCollins*Publishers*
1st Floor, Watermarque Building, Ringsend Road
Dublin 4, Ireland

This paperback edition 2022

1

First published in Great Britain in ebook format
by HarperCollins*Publishers* 2022
Copyright © Georgia Hill 2022
Georgia Hill asserts the moral right to be identified
as the author of this work
A catalogue record of this book is available from the British Library
ISBN: 978-0-00-858649-2

Printed and bound in the UK using 100% Renewable Electricity
by CPI Group (UK) Ltd

*For the ADCs. Thank you for the 'Zoom handholding.'*

The Berecombe News
**A YEAR OF COMMEMORATION**
*By: Keeley Sharma*

*This year sees the seventy-fifth anniversary of D-Day. We owe an enormous debt of gratitude to those brave American boys who went to fight on French beaches for our freedom.*

*No one can overestimate the impact of thousands of GIs arriving on our shores. Rumour has it that, even in our little town, several babies were the result of this friendly invasion and this reporter knows of at least one marriage!*

*This year the invasion is happening all over again. Berecombe is playing host to our American allies once more. All surviving soldiers who were billeted in the town and who went to Omaha Beach have been invited. New museum director Noah Lydden is co-ordinating the commemorations and says it will be a year-long feast for mind and body and, most importantly, a whole lot of fun. Street parties, special-event films, a D-Day Parade, a black-tie ball at The Henville and much, much more will be organized in and around the town.*

*So, come along, get dressed up and join in the fun!*

# Chapter One

'You can't argue with the view.' With reluctance, Ashley Lydden turned her back on the sun-soaked vista of sea and sky that was Lyme Bay and observed the tiny office instead. She smiled at her cousin fondly. Oblivious to the glorious late February day outside, Noah was hunched over his computer, his hair tousled and his brow furrowed in a look she knew well: preoccupation mixed in with a smattering of frustration. She waited patiently until he'd finished whatever it was he was doing.

Eventually he swung around on his chair. 'Ash, it's so good of you to come down and help me out with this. I'm swamped, to be honest.' He shot her a grateful look.

Ashley shrugged. 'Hey, being stuck in Ludlow with

1

the parents or a few months sunning myself in Berecombe. It's a no-brainer.' She flicked a long, dark lock of hair away from her face. 'And in between helping you organize this madly epic extravaganza, I shall attempt to do some painting. Unless I've forgotten how to do it. What on earth made you make it so complicated when you've only been in the job for five minutes?' She made her way gingerly through the muddle of papers and piles of books and sat down on the only other chair.

'I didn't. I had in mind a fairly simple verbal history project. Then the Friends of the Museum group got hold of me and put me right.' Noah grimaced. 'Apparently Berecombe is a town that likes to celebrate and the seventy-fifth anniversary of D-Day wasn't something they were going to let slip by. There's one,' he frowned, 'Biddy I think her name is – she terrifies me. I've been holed up in this office twenty-four/seven since I started the job in September. I thought it would be far too little time to organize anything big, but Biddy put me right on that. Says the town rallies. She might be right; it's got a fabulous sense of community.'

Ashley laughed. 'At least the view from your window is good. I can think of worse places to be holed up in.' She nodded to the panoramic view of the town's promenade and beach. A fresh breeze blew in and made the blind-pull flutter. It brought with it the intoxicating scent of salt-laden air.

'One advantage of being slightly up the hill and three floors up. I reckon this place has arguably the best view of any museum in the UK.' Noah winced. 'I suppose the other advantage is my thigh muscles have never been so honed.'

'No need for the gym then.'

'No time.' He groaned. 'Speaking of which, I'd better get my skates on. I'm holding an introductory memory session in twenty minutes.' He glanced at his watch. 'I'm going to have to jog.'

'Where are you headed to?'

'A café at the far end of the prom. Millie Vanilla's, I think it's called. Been in a few times. Fabulous place.'

'I know the one. Next to that fantastic bookshop.' Ashley raised her eyebrows. 'You'll have to run. It's at least half a mile. I'd jog with you, but…' She let the sentence trail.

Noah was busy collecting his handheld recorder and notebooks. 'But you can't keep up with me. Slowcoach,' he teased. Then, realizing what he'd said, he turned back to her, stricken. 'Ash, I'm so sorry. I didn't mean—'

'Will you take that look off your face! It's fine, honestly. I just have to take life at a slightly more sedate pace these days.'

'Oh lordy, Ash. I feel awful.'

'Stop it,' she said sternly. 'I developed an extremely thick skin very soon after the accident.'

'Well, look, meet me in the café later, then. I'll treat you to a coffee and an unseemly large cake to make up for my appalling lack of tact. It does the most wonderful food – one reason I chose to base the memory project there.' He came to her and dropped a kiss on the top of her head.

'And there won't be a memory project unless you go.' She pushed him playfully. 'Go!'

'See you later?'

'See you later, coz. Bye.'

Ashley didn't move. She was in no hurry to leave. She sat enjoying the view and the salty air whipping in through the window. Marshmallow clouds, the sort found in children's picture books, scurried across the pale-blue sky. Sky met sea at an almost indistinguishable horizon and everything seemed huge and open. Humbling. Since coming to Berecombe, she'd become fascinated by the sea. Its moods swung from sullen to angry and back to serenely calm, sometimes in less than an hour. She'd never tire of it. Her fingers began to itch; she wanted to get out there and paint.

She gathered her bag and straw hat and got to her

feet. Although her injuries were well on the way to being healed, everything had to be done at a slower pace these days and her balance still wasn't perfect. Thinking of the stone spiral staircase which led down from Noah's office into the museum proper, she cursed. It would take her an age to negotiate it. But she was determined to do it.

Collecting her rucksack from reception, she heaved it onto her back and made her way out into the sunshine. The museum was tucked behind the town's little theatre on a main road leading out of Berecombe, and she had to concentrate to navigate the narrow pavement thronging with tourists and too near the buses, which thundered through belching diesel. As she reached the beginning of the promenade that ran parallel to the sea and eventually led to the harbour at the other end of town, she stopped for a second and breathed a sigh of relief that she'd made it. As she did so, a man behind knocked into her.

'Oi! Watch out! Mind where you're going!' Then he passed her and caught sight of the stick. 'Oh, sorry love. Didn't see that you were...' His face shut down in embarrassment and he strode off.

Ashley steadied herself, found her balance, adjusted her rucksack's weight to the middle of her back and walked on. Since the accident there had been a shift in how people treated her. Many were kind but a few

5

displayed impatience. They'd tut as she held them up in shops, barge past her as she took up too much room on the pavement. Sometimes they even verbally abused her. For a while she'd stopped venturing out alone. Eventually, though, pride and frustration conquered the fear and she began going solo again.

Her parents hated it, terrified she was vulnerable to attack, or that she would fall and be unable to get help. Their concern, although she knew it came from a place of love, was suffocating. It was what had driven her to accept Noah's request. That and the offer of the self-contained flat in the house he was renting near the centre of town, which had reasonable bus links and the promise of, if not paid work at the museum, then something to keep her mind occupied.

Her parents, reluctantly agreeing to the plan, had driven her down in a car stuffed with belongings. She'd tried not to laugh; it was a sad parody of when they'd driven her to teacher training college a decade ago. Her father had sniffed around the flat, grudgingly agreed it would do, being on one level, and then had examined it for trip hazards. Her mother, having stocked up the freezer with Tupperware boxes of home-cooked meals, had fretted about whether her daughter would cope. Ashley had squeezed her tight, reassured her she'd be fine and reminded her that she had Noah on the floor above just in case. They'd eventually got into the Jag and disappeared. They were breaking the journey back at a country hotel and Ashley hoped they'd have a chance to relax. Since the accident everything had been full-on and she knew they were exhausted. She loved her parents and was deeply grateful to them for the care they'd taken of her while she recuperated, but living with them had been teeth-gnashingly awful. She'd reverted to being a moody teenager – only worse. She wasn't proud of how she'd behaved and her parents hadn't deserved it. After waving the car off, she'd shut her own private front door, leaned against it and breathed in sea air and freedom.

And now, scanning Berecombe promenade for an empty bench facing out to sea, she spied one in the distance. Trying not to hurry before it was taken, she concentrated on walking properly, as the physios had taught her. Back straight, consciously feeling the concrete beneath each part of her foot as it made contact and making sure she had both feet facing forwards. Her shattered pelvic girdle had meant she had needed to learn to walk again and, even now, when she was tired, her left leg dragged a little. Not today though. Unless you were looking closely, you wouldn't notice anything amiss. Apart from the stick, of course, and Ashley hoped she'd be able to ditch that soon. By some miracle, seeing as the town was busy with spring sunshine-seeking tourists, the bench was still vacant when she got to it. She collapsed onto it gratefully. It was the furthest she'd walked since arriving in Berecombe. Lifting her head to the sky, she drank in the warm sunshine and relished being alive.

## Chapter Two

Ashley began her routine. Putting her rucksack on the bench beside her, she took off her straw hat, wedging the brim under her bag so it wouldn't blow away. She tied a scarf around her hair. The whisper of bluey-green silk stopped it blowing into her eyes while she worked and, along with giant sunglasses, hid the scar which ran livid behind her ear. She rested her watercolour pad on her lap and took out her travelling paint tin. She regretted not being able to bring an easel but just couldn't carry it along with her rucksack and stick, needing her hands free should she fall. The little tin of Windsor and Newton paints, her plastic jar of water and pad did the job until she could get home to paint on something larger. It was like taking visual notes before working them into the final piece and worked well for her. Stowing the stick inside the rucksack, she thanked the heavens that the latest incumbent was collapsible. Her little ritual performed, she surveyed the coastline with pleasure, taking in the solemn grey Blue Lias cliffs and the fossil hunters scrabbling over the rocks in an attempt to find a scrap of ammonite or belemnite. The Lias bled into the fiery red of the sandstone at West Bay which then, in turn, seeped into the blinding white of Portland. She made a mental note to look up what buses could get her there; she'd love to visit but driving was out of the equation at the moment. Ashley had become entranced by this stretch of coastline.

Aware someone had sat at the other end of the bench, she shifted her body away and towards the view. She hoped the signal was clear: *Do not disturb*. Meeting new people could be fraught, as she was forced to explain yet again why she walked with a stick. It could be exhausting. Today she simply wanted to concentrate on painting. Too few people took heed of body language, but to her relief, this particular person took the hint.

She began to work, ignoring the tourists walking past on the promenade and the traffic on the road which ran parallel. For a while she used pencil and made some rapid-fire marks, enjoying the rasp of pencil on paper. She'd discovered she attracted less attention when drawing. For some reason a vividly painted watercolour drew a crowd and she was still getting used to the attention. A cloud drifted over the sun, transforming the scene into something with softer shades, something more subtle, and she worked even quicker to capture the change in light. The breeze got up, making the cloud blow off to the east. Immediately everything became bright yellow and turquoise again. It was too much of a temptation. Flicking over to a new page, she dipped her brush into water and began to paint.

Eventually, as her back was getting stiff, she stopped. She was just about to put away her kit when a car horn split the peace. It was followed by the sickening crunch of metal grinding on metal. Shouts. Aggressive swearing. Ashley flinched so violently, her pad slipped from her fingers and the water jar rolled to the ground, scattering brushes. Concentrating on her breathing, she screwed her eyes shut. Counting backwards in her head, she became aware of a voice to her right. A man. An American accent.

'Aw jeez, you've dropped your things. Here, let me.'

Ashley opened her eyes to see a man crouching on the sandy concrete, gathering up her painting things in his big hands. He rose to sit beside her. Too traumatized to take much in, she caught a flash of humorous eyes in a friendly face.

'Shall I put them in your bag?'

'No!' The response came out sharper than intended. Softening, she explained, 'It has to go in a certain way or it won't all fit.'

'Okay.'

He sat patiently while she opened the rucksack. He made no comment on her trembling, clumsy hands or the stick which she took out, extended and laid on the bench between them.

'Just tell me what you need first,' he said equably. Handing things over in the order she requested, he kept up a running commentary about the accident behind them. 'Looks like just a shunt,' he said. 'No real damage except to the trunk. Two young guys, by the look of things. Got to the stage of exchanging numbers now. All calmed down.' He handed her the now empty water jar, having first screwed on the lid. 'Sounded worse than it is, I guess. Often does when cars hit one another.'

'Not always.' Ashley took the watercolour pad from him and slid it into its slot. She zipped up the rucksack but made no attempt to move. She didn't trust her legs quite yet.

'You know, you look very pale. Can I get someone for you? Or take you for a coffee?' He spread his hands. 'Look, this isn't a pick-up line, I promise. I was headed for one anyway.'

Ashley shook her head. 'No, I'm fine.'

'You sure?'

'I am absolutely all right. I just want to sit here for a minute.'

'Well, okay, but I hate leaving you like this.' He rose and went to go, then stopped and turned back to her. 'You got a cell?'

'A what?' she blinked up at him, wishing he would go away and leave her in peace. He was very tall and his bulk was silhouetted against the light.

'A phone. A mobile.'

'Oh, yes.'

'And you're sure I can't call someone for you?'

She shook her head. 'No thank you. I'm meeting someone soon. I'll just sit here for a while and enjoy the sun.'

He was obviously reluctant to leave. 'Well, if you're sure.'

'I am. Thank you. You've been most kind.' Even to her ears it came out ridiculously prim and middle-class English. She just wanted him gone.

'Right. Have a good day then. I'll maybe see you around. I'm discovering Berecombe is a small town. Everyone seems to know one another.'

'Quite possibly.'

He gave a nod, turned on his heel and left.

Ashley couldn't hide her relief that she was alone. Closing her eyes, she leaned back on the bench and soaked up the sun's warmth. Eventually her breathing became regulated and she felt a semblance of normality return.

## Chapter Three

S he was going to be late. Slipping on her rucksack, she got up, stretched her stiff left leg and began to make her way towards the café where Noah suggested they should meet.

The sun was slipping down in the sky and, with the heat gone out of the day, it felt more like normal February temperatures. She'd be glad of a coffee or hot chocolate. The promenade curved round and, just before the harbour proper began, the café and its adjoining bookshop hove into view, with its wide-open space stretching in front and jutting out into the beach. A low wall separated the seating area from the beach, and tables and benches were crowded with customers.

Ashley had visited the bookshop already. She'd enjoyed browsing the art section and the books on display to celebrate the upcoming film festival at the local theatre. Resisting the very tempting but incredibly expensive coffee-table tome on Jean Cocteau, she'd settled on a fat best-selling paperback. One of the positive things about her new life was having the time to read. She paused for a second before going into the café. New situations, new people, weren't as easy to navigate as they once were. Then, taking a deep breath, she walked through the bifold doors and into the café proper.

It was crowded. The air, heavy with the seductive scent of vanilla, coffee and sugar, was somehow reminiscent of childhood days baking with her mother. There was a low hum of happy chatter from the customers sitting at tables painted in mismatched pastel ice-cream colours. Clashing with the colour scheme was the mass of red, white and blue bunting strung from the walls and abundant across the ceiling. 'Don't Sit Under the Apple Tree', jaunty and in close harmony, sang out from the sound system. Someone was embracing all things 1940s. It added up to being warm and welcoming and felt like walking into the best kind of hug from a very good friend.

'Ashley, we're over here.' It was Noah. 'I've saved you a seat.' As she squeezed her way through the jumble of chairs and tables, he added, 'You're late, but just in time for a second round of coffee and cake. Sit down and I'll order, and then introduce you to everyone. Petra,' he called to a petite woman with a blonde-bombshell hairdo tied up in a red spotted scarf, 'can we get another round of what we had before, plus lemon drizzle and a latte for my darling coz.'

Petra grinned, nodded and then disappeared through the swing door, which was complete with a porthole window, and into what Ashley assumed was the kitchen.

Once she'd settled into her seat, she sent a nervous smile round to everyone. Noah took the cue. 'This is Biddy,' he said. It was only because she knew her cousin well that she detected the briefest of winks. So this was the woman who was causing him so much trouble. 'Hello,' she said, taking in an impression of iron-grey hair flattened by a purple beret, and a pair of fearsome black eyebrows.

Biddy nodded back. 'Pleased to meet you, I'm sure.' She hoisted a tiny black dog onto her lap. 'And this is Elvis, my deaf-assistance dog. I'm hard of hearing, you see.'

Ashley liked dogs and wanted to pat the scrap of black poodle but wasn't sure if it was allowed.

Biddy read her mind. 'It's acceptable to stroke a deaf-assistance dog even when working. It's different with guide dogs. That's not allowed under any circumstances,' she added, as Ashley reached out a hand for the poodle to sniff. 'But I'd rather you didn't. He is working, after all.'

Ashley snatched her hand back. That told her. Aware that Noah was stifling a laugh, she said sharply, 'And please introduce me to your other friends, Noah.'

'Of course.' Sobering, he said, 'This is Beryl. A Friend of the Museum, as is Biddy.'

'Hello my lovely,' said a woman in, perhaps, her seventies. She was much more approachable-looking with her cropped silver hair, vivid yellow linen smock and dangly earrings.

'And this is Ken Tizzard,' Noah continued. 'He runs Berecombe Arts Workshop. You'll have to take a look, Ash. Ashley is an art teacher and paints,' he explained to the middle-aged man sitting next to Beryl.

'Well, I used to teach art,' Ashley explained quickly. 'Not any longer, but I still like to paint.'

'Once the art gets you, that's it. That's my experience,' Ken said. He had a strong Devon accent with soft, rolling 'r's. 'You'd be welcome any time. We're just beyond the tennis courts. Not the prettiest part of town but not far from the centre. Come and have a look.'

'Thank you, I will.' Biddy aside, they seemed friendly. 'How has the first session gone?'

'Bit of a disaster,' Noah admitted. 'We had a Mr

Senior telling us all about his allotment, and Katrina Chilcombe went on about how miserable Berecombe was when she was a teenager growing up in the seventies and how she couldn't wait to escape. It wasn't quite what I had in mind.'

'Ennis Senior could bore for England,' Biddy put in. 'And Katrina Chilcombe only came for the free coffee and cake. She's Amy's mother,' she explained to Ashley. 'Amy runs the bookshop but is definitely cut from different cloth to her mother. Chalk and cheese, those two.'

'Oh Biddy, be kind,' said Beryl. 'Ennis is lonely since he lost his wife and Katrina has had her disappointments. I find them both charming.'

Biddy sniffed. 'You'd find Hitler charming if he made you a sandwich.'

'Well,' Noah began, obviously unsure of what to say. 'Oh look,' he added, relieved. 'Here comes our cake order.' Standing up, he beamed at a frazzled Petra. 'Can I do anything to help?'

'Cool, thanks Noah. You're a star. I'm run off my feet this afternoon. Could you hand round the cakes while I serve the teas and coffees?'

He did so, getting everyone's order wrong. No one seemed to mind, not even Biddy. Noah had that scarce but highly prized quality of likeability. Ashley observed with amusement as he handed Beryl some coffee and walnut cake, only for her to swap it for Ken's buttered teabread slice. If her cousin had one failing, if you could even call it such, he suffered from an over-abundance of enthusiasm. It could get quite exhausting keeping up with him sometimes. Once everyone had finally received their correct order and the drinks had been served, Ashley watched as he and Petra exchanged looks and Petra blushed a little. That was Noah's other talent; he had effortless charm.

Petra put the empty tray under her arm and rushed off.

'Is Petra the owner of the café?' Ashley asked, as she took a sip of her latte, needing its warmth and the caffeine kick.

'Of course not,' Biddy answered. 'That's Millie Fudge, or should I say Millie Henville now, since she got married. She got married right here on the beach. As my darling Arthur and I did. Winter weddings both. It was perfect. And then it snowed and made it even more perfect.'

'When's the baby due?' Beryl asked, nibbling at an edge of teabread.

For a bizarre second Ashley thought Beryl meant Biddy's baby. The woman must be well into her seventies.

'Late June, I was told,' Biddy answered. 'Although you can never tell with first babies. They like to hang on a bit.'

'Going to be such a pretty baby, what with Millie and Jed as parents. Are they still living in that lovely old cottage in the valley? The Greys's old place.'

'They are,' Biddy went on importantly. 'Went over to have afternoon tea last week. Wonderful little spot. And your Emma's still in the flat above the caff, isn't she, Ken?'

'That's my niece,' he explained to Ashley. 'You'll find everyone in Berecombe is either related or knows one another.'

As if to prove his point, a familiar American voiced sounded. 'Hi there,' he called. 'Glad you found your friends and got that coffee.'

Ashley looked up. It was the man from the bench. This time he was facing into the light so she could see him better. Swept-back golden-brown hair, a strong chin and jaw, eyes lit with an easy humour. Handsome. Confident. Maybe overly so.

'You two know one another?' Noah said, sizing him up. 'Pray do tell.' He stood up.

Ashley, sensing Noah was out to cause mischief, said hurriedly, 'I spilled my painting kit all over the prom and this kind person helped me pick it all up.' She stopped, wondering if the stranger was going to embarrass her and regale them all with the tale of her panic attack.

'Eddie. Eddie McQueen.' He offered Noah his hand and they shook.

'Not *the* Eddie McQueen? From Southwestern University? The social history expert?'

'The very same.'

'I'm Noah Lydden. I run the museum here. Good to meet you.'

'Ah, great to meet you too, Noah. I've been meaning to mosey over to the museum and introduce myself.'

'Please do. We'd be honoured to have you.'

Ashley was intrigued. Noah looked starstruck. Whoever this Eddie McQueen was, he must be someone important.

Eddie turned to her. 'I was only too glad to be of service.' His gaze was penetrating. 'I couldn't help but admire your work, Miss... erm...?'

'Ashley. I'm Ashley Lydden. Hello again.'

'Well, hi there, Ashley.' Eddie smiled, showing perfect American teeth. 'Delighted to meet you properly.' There was a beat between them before he added, 'I'm on my way for a takeout. Best coffee in town. Best I've had this side of the Atlantic, even.'

'It's certainly good.' Ashley felt her face flame and cursed herself. What was she? Fourteen?

Noah sat down again. 'Eddie, would you like to join us?' He spread his hands as an introduction to the rest of the group.

'Thank you for the kind invitation, but I'm heading off for my train. Another time maybe?'

'Another time,' Noah said on a grin, casting a sly look Ashley's way. 'I'm sure you'd be *very* welcome. And don't forget to pop by the museum when you've got the chance.'

'I'll be sure to do that.'

Ashley resisted the urge to kick Noah. She felt Eddie's eyes on her and her cheeks bloomed even further.

'Be seeing you.' And then he was gone as suddenly as he had appeared.

'Well now,' boomed Biddy. 'I think someone has made herself a conquest!'

Noah eyed his cousin curiously. 'I rather think someone has.'

## Chapter Four

This time Ashley did kick him. To change the subject, she asked, 'You know, I'm still not sure exactly how this memory project is going to work.'

Beryl put her teacup down with a delicate chink. 'Oh Ashley, I'm glad you said that. Neither am I, to be honest.'

Biddy huffed. 'You were at the first Friends meeting when we all discussed it,' she snapped. 'Just what precisely don't you understand?'

Beryl flapped her hands, making her dangly earrings join in. 'You know, I'm not clear on the details.' She turned to Biddy with a gleam in her eye, making Ashley like her even more. 'Perhaps *you* can outline how it's all going to happen?'

'Well,' Biddy began. 'Folk'll tell us their memories and I suppose we'll record them.' She tailed off, looking embarrassed, and huffed again. 'I'll let Noah fill you in.'

'Glad to,' he said genially. 'As you know, there'll be a comprehensive programme of events throughout the year. We've been busy mailing out invitations to any American soldiers who were billeted here and we have host families willing to put them up. The Henville is offering a discounted rate for those preferring a little luxury, or they can stay in a home environment.'

'They'll be quite old by now, won't they?' Ashley put in.

'They will. The youngest will be in their early nineties, I suppose. That's why we need to take special care of them.'

'That and the fact that they're heroes,' Biddy put in.

'Indeed,' Noah said. 'I'm liaising with a contact at the 16th Infantry Regimental Association and I want to make the visit absolutely right. We'll have a welcoming tea party, weather permitting, and a dinner dance at The Henville. Plus other events if I can get them sorted.'

'Will they take part in the memory project?' Beryl asked. She grimaced. 'It might be painful for them.'

'They can, if they want to, although I take on board it might rake up some difficult stuff. I'd like to concentrate on their time here in Berecombe and their interaction with the community, rather than what they experienced when they went to Omaha.'

'I don't know about raking up the memories,' Biddy said. 'I expect they've never forgotten them.'

'Agree there, Biddy,' Ken put in. 'Post combat stress disorder isn't a recent invention.'

'I understand about getting people to record their memories,' Beryl said, with a frown. 'But what are you going to do with it all?'

Noah turned to her with a smile. 'I'd like to add a selection of memories to the museum's archives. We can keep them as recordings or transcribe them, if we want. I rather think hearing what's said in the speaker's own voice would be more powerful.'

'Mmm. Unless it's Ennis Senior and his endless tales from his allotment,' Biddy said as she picked up Elvis and fed him the remaining crumbs from her scone.

Beryl laughed. 'You are wicked, Biddy.'

'She's got a point though,' Ken added.

'There'll be a certain amount of judicious editing to be done. We can't record anything and everything. And once it's all complete, I plan to put on an exhibition.' Noah lifted a hopeful eyebrow at Ken.

'Yes, you can use the centre.' Ken shrugged. 'It's what it's for, my friend.'

'How's an exhibition of voices going to work?' Ashley asked.

'We can play the recordings through headphones or have audio to accompany visuals in soundproof sections. Lots of museums use audio-visual in that way.' Noah drained his coffee. 'Actually, coz, I've another idea I want to run past you.'

'Figures.' Ashley pulled a face. 'What do you want me to do?'

'Do you still have that all-singing, all-dancing, makes-toast camera?'

'The Nikon? Yes. Why?'

'I'd love some photographs to add into the exhibition mix. We've lots of archive material but I'd like some modern images of the town too. Plus some portraits of those taking part in the memory project.'

'I'll have a go,' Ashley said, slowly. 'I'm a bit rusty though, and portraiture was never my strong point.'

'You'll have to put a bit of practice in then, my friend.' Ken gurned. 'Start with me?'

Ashley laughed. She was beginning to like Ken. 'You're on.'

He stood up. 'And now, I have to get back to work or the wife will, quite rightly, have my knackers for earrings if I'm late home again.'

They all said goodbye and then Beryl and Biddy made 'got to go' noises too.

'Come on, Beryl, old girl,' Biddy said as she helped the woman up. 'Stir your stumps. Best get you to the square or you won't make your bus.'

'Old girl indeed,' Beryl replied waspishly. She poked Biddy in the back. 'Get on with you. I've got barely five years on you.' She turned to Noah and Ashley. 'Useful session, Noah, and lovely to meet you, Ashley.'

With a flurry of putting on coats and scarves, they left.

'So,' Noah said, fixing his eyes on Ashley. 'This Eddie McQueen. *The* Eddie McQueen. Tell all.'

'There is absolutely nothing to tell.'

'Well, as soon as there is, remember I have to vet all possible candidates.'

'I don't think Eddie McQueen will be a candidate for anything,' Ashley replied, firmly. To shut the conversation down further, she added, 'I have two questions for you, actually.'

'Which are?'

'How on earth are you going to cope with Biddy?'

Noah sniggered in a juvenile manner which completely belied his thirty-four years. 'I shall use the famous Lydden charm,' he said airily. 'Never failed me yet. Second question?'

Ashley glanced over to the café counter where the glamorous Petra was manning the till. 'Just what's going on between you and the fragrant café manager?'

That shut him up.

## Chapter Five

Ashley loved the independence her flat gave her. On the ground floor of the house Noah was renting, it was small but cosy and even had its own sun terrace. It was the perfect retreat to hide in when things got too much, when the pain in her healing limbs couldn't be controlled, when the exhaustion of getting out and facing the world overcame her. She was still taking baby steps and had underestimated how cocooned she'd been when with her parents. Starting a new chapter of her life in this welcoming seaside town had been what she wanted, and craved, but it took effort. Some days she simply wanted to hide and force away the hideous, nightmare-ish flashbacks to the accident. On the worst days, Noah had been a star – dropping by, making no comment but bringing a takeaway or making an enormous pot of tea and tucking the duvet around her as she slumped on the sofa in front of the television.

On good days, he joined her with a takeout curry and they chatted about her hopes for the future. Ashley wanted to find some kind of job; she'd never been good at being idle. She was desperate to paint more. She hankered after a community and missed being part of one.

A routine emerged. The weather stayed unseasonably warm and dry, and she took to going out at dawn and enjoying the solitude the early hour afforded. She recharged the battery on her camera and began taking practice shots. She'd been right, she was rusty, but with Berecombe providing such stunning light, it was difficult to go far wrong. A detail of a wrought-iron railing, double yellow lines shimmering in a puddle, a pebble glossed by seawater and the reflection of a pink sunrise caught in a windowpane. She snapped anything that caught her eye.

The escape Berecombe afforded was gradually eroding the brittle façade she'd constructed in order to face the world. She was beginning to relax.

There were usually few others about, except for dog walkers. Ashley couldn't resist stopping and fussing some dogs and became fond of the regulars she came across. One morning rain prevented her from going out quite as early and, as she was walking along the promenade towards the café, she saw a familiar figure in front of her. The purple beret and the tiny black poodle prancing at her heels told her who it was. She slowed, waiting to see where Biddy was going. Ashley craved a bacon sandwich and a big mug of hot chocolate and knew Millie Vanilla's would be the place to get them. It was obviously where Biddy was heading too, as she continued to march towards the café and strode purposefully inside. Ashley had loved meeting them all in the café but didn't feel like company this morning. Sometimes, putting on the face with which she braved the public was too much effort. Then she pulled herself together; the thought of hot chocolate and a bacon butty dripping with brown sauce overrode her reluctance to encounter Biddy. It was time to change. She was determined.

As soon as she walked in, the woman called over and ordered her to join her at the table in the window. 'Always the best table in the house,' she boomed. 'Especially at this time of year. I like to watch people walking past looking frozen.'

'It's been warm though, hasn't it, for February?' Ashley ventured. 'Or is it always mild down here at this time of year?'

'Can be. Or there can be a wind that comes off the sea

that slices your head off. "Ne'er cast a clout 'til May be out", my mother always used to say.'

Ashley didn't answer. She hadn't a clue what that meant.

As Petra, immaculate in bright-red lipstick and matching nails, approached their table, Biddy barked out, 'My usual, please.'

'Certainly, Biddy. Coffee and a scone coming up. And Ashley, what can I get you?'

Ashley put in her order, impressed that Petra had remembered her name.

As soon as Petra had gone, Biddy turned her siren gaze onto her. 'So, young Ashley, what have you been up to?'

Ashley held up the camera in answer.

'And what have you been taking pictures of?'

'Everything and anything. Getting used to the camera again, to be honest.'

Biddy peered at it as if it were an alien being. 'Is it one of those fancy digital things?'

'Yes.' Ashley switched it on and showed her the viewfinder. 'It stores the images on an SD card and I download them onto my laptop so I can view what I've taken properly and edit out the duds.'

Biddy peered into the small square. 'I don't know how you can see what you've taken on that thing.'

'It is tricky, to be honest,' Ashley admitted. 'Especially when I'm shooting into strong light. I have to confess to snapping away and then sifting through them at home. I quite enjoy it, seeing what the image looks like properly. The editing software is very effective too, although I'm on a steep learning curve at the moment.'

'Very impressive, I'm sure.'

'I think Noah wants portraits of the people taking part in the memory project.' Ashley grimaced. 'I'll have to bone up on portrait photography. I don't know anything about that.'

'I've got a contact. In London. He might be able to help.'

'Thank you,' Ashley said, taken aback at this unexpected offer of help. 'I'd really appreciate that.'

'Mind you, this photographer I knew from back in the 60s, he had the proper stuff. SLR, you know. I remember it was a Leica. Darkroom, chemicals and an enlarger and suchlike. The works. He used to photograph models. Twiggy and Jean Shrimpton. It was like magic watching the pictures emerge from the developing tray. Standing in the pitch dark.' A wistful look came over Biddy's face. 'I can still smell the developing fluid now. I used to have a Biba minidress, lime-green gingham it was, with a cut-out panel on each side and a white plastic belt around the hips. I used to have a proper waist and hips back then.'

She wriggled her nose and then said in matter-of-fact tones, 'Well, that's brought a few memories back, an' all.'

Ashley was intrigued at the thought of Biddy as a young woman, moving in such fashionable circles. He must have been a talented and successful photographer to have Twiggy as a model. 'Was he a boyfriend? Of yours, I mean?'

'Not exactly a boyfriend, no.' Biddy pursed her lips, indicating the subject was closed.

The awkward silence was rescued by Petra bringing them their food. Ashley relaxed a little as a steaming mug of chocolate and a roll rich with juicy bacon was put in front of her. Perhaps sharing breakfast with Biddy wasn't going to be the ordeal she'd feared.

'So,' Biddy said, as she spread her scone liberally with some creamy yellow butter. 'Why do you walk with that thing?' She nodded at the stick hooked onto the back of Ashley's chair.

Ashley put down the bacon roll abruptly, chewing the mouthful she'd just taken. Swallowing with difficulty, as a lump had suddenly formed in her throat, she considered her answer. This was why it was so difficult meeting new people; she had to go through the rigmarole of deciding what to say and how much to reveal. It had become tedious. Glancing at Biddy, who was staring back with open but not malevolent curiosity, she decided it couldn't do any harm to tell her. It would get it out of the way.

'I was in a car accident,' she began slowly. 'I suffered some pretty serious injuries and it took a while to get better.' She shrugged. 'I decided I didn't want to teach any longer so, you see, I'm at a bit of a crossroads. I'm taking some time to think through what next to do with my life.'

'Ah.'

Ashley picked out a sliver of crispy bacon and ate it.

'Not on that A35?' Biddy asked, referring to one of the main east–west routes through Dorset and Devon. 'The accident I mean. Death trap, that road.'

'No, it was in Shropshire. Where my family are from.' *Where I used to live and work,* Ashley added in her head. Her old life seemed a long time ago and as if it had happened to a different person. That much was true. She had been a different person to the one she was now. Pre- and post-accident life had a strict demarcation line.

Biddy crumbled off a morsel of scone and her hand disappeared from view. Presumably she was feeding it to Elvis. 'And what happened in this car accident?' she asked.

Ashley sensed a softening, an unexpected kindness. Biddy was proving an excellent listener. 'It was an old car. Everyone kept on at me to trade it in for something newer, a bit more reliable, but most of the time it only had to get me into and back from school, so I kept it going. I had great plans to travel that summer holiday and didn't want to spend all my savings on a new car. My boyfriend and I wanted to do India.' She bit her lip. 'That was a mistake.'

'The car or the man?'

'Both, as it turned out.' Ashley shook her head slightly. 'The car broke down and—'

'And?'

'And a lorry ran into it.'

'Oh, my dear girl.' Biddy put a comforting hand on top of Ashley's. She tutted and shook her head, obviously shocked. 'And it's left you walking with a stick? What was he doing? On his phone, I expect, or dozing off and not concentrating.'

'Yes, the police suspected he was texting.'

'I sincerely hope it's left the driver without a job,' Biddy said robustly.

It had certainly left Ashley without a job.

Her recovery had been slow and hard won. At first she hadn't been able to stand for any length of time, which meant teaching was more or less impossible. But the decision to resign had less to do with physical restrictions than the destruction of all of her self-confidence. She had gone from being on the verge of being made departmental head and enjoying all that life had to offer, to being, at least at the beginning, totally reliant on her parents. She'd had no choice but to move back into their comfortable house in Ludlow. Her friends visited less and less. They made it apparent that visiting was a chore and she increasingly felt she no longer had anything in common with them. Or perhaps she never had? They were full of stories of seeing the latest film, going to a new bar that had opened, the fantastic weekend they'd just spent in Barcelona, and all she had to talk about was endless hospital visits and physio. The demarcation line had formed quickly and the visits had tailed off.

'And this boyfriend? Has he stuck by you?'

Ashley squared her shoulders and picked up her bacon roll. 'Piers? He drifted away. He tried to be supportive, I suppose, in his way.' She took a mouthful and chewed. 'But he was into his surfing and his snow-boarding.' She gave a grim laugh. 'A girlfriend who was learning to walk again wasn't really his scene. I cramped his style somewhat.'

'In which case,' Biddy said matter-of-factly, 'he's done you a favour. You don't need a man like that in your life. Although it probably didn't seem like it at that moment.'

Ashley took another bite. The roll was delicious, and for some reason, she felt hugely better sharing her sorry tale with Biddy. Who would have thought? Finishing her breakfast, she wiped her fingers on the bright pink paper serviette and agreed. Piers' good-looking face swam into her vision. It had taken the accident to make her realize how totally superficial and arrogant he was. And how little they had in common. 'You may well have a point there, Biddy.'

'I usually do.' The old woman looked around. 'And now, if I can ever get Petra's attention, after all that soul-searching I think we deserve cake.' She glanced at Ashley's empty mug. 'And more hot chocolate?'

Ashley grinned. 'Why not?'

## Chapter Six

O ver another scone for Biddy and an enormous slice of coffee and walnut cake for Ashley (who, after a bacon roll and two hot chocolates laden with cream and marshmallows, had long given up the fight against calories), they chatted some more. Biddy told her about the bungalow she and her husband had just bought and which needed a lot of work, and mentioned living in London for most of her life.

'But what about you, young Ashley? Will you settle in Berecombe or return to Ludlow? It's a beautiful town.'

'And a beautiful county too.' Ashley scooped out an errant marshmallow. 'I'm down here, supposedly helping Noah out, but to be honest, I hardly see him. He's always in meetings.' She shuddered a little. 'Not my idea of the perfect job. I find meetings incredibly tedious.'

Biddy smirked. 'Usually a collection of men sitting around pontificating and shaking their peacock feathers. My poor Arthur is a town councillor, don't you know, and he has his fair share of meetings to attend.'

'I'm seeing this as an opportunity to decide what I really want to do,' Ashley said thoughtfully, as if fully realizing it for the first time. 'I'll be due some compensation once the solicitors have stopped wrangling, so I'll have a bit to stash away, and Noah's not charging me any rent. It's given me the freedom to decide how I want to spend the rest of my life.'

Biddy made a kind of hurrumphing noise. 'In my considerable experience, as soon as you decide what you want to do in life, it always throws you a curve ball, making you re-think it all over again. Live for today is my advice, maybe next week at a stretch.'

'Sounds like a good philosophy,' Ashley laughed. 'But I've got to decide some things.'

'Such as?'

'Where to live. What work to do. I can't not work.'

'Would you consider going back into teaching?'

'Maybe. But possibly not in the same way.'

'Could you make a living out of your paintings? I

haven't seen your work but I remember that American chappie saying how good he thought you were.'

'I might be able to.' Ashley pushed her mug away. One more sugar-laden calorie and she'd burst. 'Not sure I'm good enough.' She flicked a look at Biddy. 'To be honest, I wouldn't have the first idea how to get a painting career off the ground.'

'If I was you I'd pop by the Arts Workshop and have a chat to Ken. He's been doing what he does most of his life and he knows the local art scene like no one else. He'd be my first port of call.'

'I will. Thank you, Biddy.' Ashley paused. 'Thank you for everything.'

'Stuff and nonsense, girl. I was just an ear.'

Ashley grinned. The woman had been so much more. It had been cathartic to talk to her. 'If you'll just excuse me, I have to go to the loo.'

Biddy picked up her copy of the local paper and opened it. 'Just over there, door on the left,' she barked.

When Ashley returned, Biddy was engrossed in the newspaper, so she began to collect her things, having paid Petra. She'd paid for Biddy's coffee and scones too; it seemed the least she could do. She'd been bemused at Petra's reaction.

'That's a lovely thing to do, but you don't need to do that for the old girl,' she'd said. 'Didn't you know she's worth an absolute fortune? She could buy you a year's worth of cake and it wouldn't even dent her savings.'

Ashley had returned to the table wondering just what it was that Biddy had done in London.

'I'll be off then, Biddy,' she said, winding her scarf around her neck. 'It's been really nice spending time with you. I'd like to do it again.'

'Yes. Whatever. Or as Arthur's granddaughter puts it, "Whatevs".' Biddy scowled. 'Dreadful phrase. Don't know where she picks them up from, and she's at university too. Or "uni", as she insists on referring to it. Fat lot of good an expensive education is doing her. Sit back down a minute, will you. There's something in the paper I think you ought to read.'

Ashley sat obediently and read the article Biddy pointed out. It was brief and to the point. A local man, James Larcombe, had recently died in Fir Tree Hall, Berecombe's nursing home. He'd achieved the grand age of a hundred and one and had been a much-loved member of the home, popular with the care staff. 'All very sad, Biddy, but—'

'You don't see the point in knowing about it.'

'Well, yes.'

'What if I said Jimmy Larcombe had lived in the town all of his life, that he spent his spare time helping out in the lifeboat shop, worked all of his life for the town council.' Biddy leaned forward to emphasize her point. 'That he was a war hero?'

'I'd say it was a life well lived.'

'And what if I told you he's got no one, not one soul, to see him off to his next life?'

'I'd say that was very sad.'

'More than sad, it's a bloody disgrace. A man like that, and no one there to see him buried!'

'Did he never marry, have a family?'

Biddy shook her head. 'All I know is, he had his heart broken and never found anyone else who matched up.'

'But what about the council and the lifeboat shop – won't they send representatives?'

Biddy huffed. 'Might do, but Jimmy served on both over forty years ago. Besides, it's not like having your family around, is it?'

'No, you're right, it isn't.' Ashley sat back. 'There is something we could try – I could try,' she began slowly.

'And what's that?'

'It's something I've seen done before. You put out an appeal on social media, in the press, on the TV.'

'To do what?'

'Asking if anyone knew Mr Larcombe or might be related to him. And if they'd like to attend the funeral.' Ashley sat up, suddenly enthused. 'With the internet, the world is so small nowadays, and people are so far flung, you could reach – oh, I don't know – a grandson living in Australia or a cousin in the States easily.'

'Might have to be a great-grandson,' Biddy observed tartly. 'Old Jimmy was over a hundred. And besides, to have grandchildren, don't you need to have children? Jimmy had neither, to my knowledge.'

'Yes, I suppose so. That hadn't occurred to me. Great-great nephews and nieces then. I'm assuming most, if not all of his contemporaries have died too. Any friends of his generation would be long gone. But we may be able to trace younger relatives.'

'Sounds like a lot of work.'

'It might be. It might just be a case of setting up a Facebook page, going on Twitter, maybe contacting the local papers. It's the sort of human-interest story they love. You say he was a war hero?'

'Dunkirk, I've been told.'

'Well, that's perfect,' Ashley cried. 'It sort of fits in with Noah's museum project too. I might be able to do it with the museum's blessing, and I quite like a challenge.'

'You might not be able to find anyone,' Biddy warned.

'True.' Ashley stood up, galvanized. 'But if that's the case, Noah and I will go to the funeral. You too, Biddy, and perhaps your Arthur as a council representative, and I'm sure I can get someone from the lifeboat station to come along. There'll be the care home staff too.' She grinned. 'Whatever happens, we'll give James a Berecombe funeral to be proud of!'

'That's my girl. And there's you wondering what you were going to do with your time,' Biddy said, with a curious gleam in her eye.

'I did, didn't I! And now I have a project all of my own. Thanks, Biddy. Thank you so much. Let's do this again, shall we? Meet up for a coffee, I mean.'

'You're on. And now,' Biddy added, nodding to the door, 'hadn't you better get cracking? The funeral's two weeks on Wednesday.'

Ashley shrugged on her coat, a flush of excitement brightening her cheek. 'I'd better, hadn't I? Lots to do!'

Biddy watched her go, walking carefully but with determination along the promenade. She picked up Elvis and tickled him under the chin. 'Went like clockwork, didn't it?' she said with the satisfied air of someone who had done a job well. Tugging gently on his black woolly ear, she added, 'Young Ashley just needed purpose in her life, didn't she, my boy? And now she's got it.'

## Chapter Seven

The week passed in a blur. Ashley couldn't believe the response she got from the Facebook page she put up, and from her Twitter feed. Hundreds got in touch. Replies varied from those expressing regret that such a man was in danger of being buried with few to mourn him, to people who thought they may have known Jimmy and wanted more information. Lots more documented the part their own relatives played in the war. She printed out most of them and began sticking them into a book, thinking it could go on display at the funeral and then, maybe, in the museum. She was kept busy and any early morning jaunts to take photographs were put on hold.

One evening, as Ashley was sifting through a raft of

emails and sorting the genuine from the inevitable oddballs, she was surprised to hear her doorbell ring.

Her head reared up. She knew no one in Berecombe who was likely to pay her a visit. Noah, she knew, was at yet another meeting and wouldn't bother ringing the bell anyway. He usually just yelled through the letterbox.

Getting up stiffly, not realizing how long she'd been poring over the computer, she went into her tiny hall and peered through the spy-hole. A tall man stood on her doorstep, his light-brown hair gleaming in the streetlight. It was Eddie McQueen. Swinging open the door, she blinked and said, without thinking, 'Noah's out I'm afraid, if that's who you want.'

He grinned, creating a deep groove down one side of his mouth that was very sexy. 'Hi, Ashley. Actually, it's not Noah I'm after. It's you.'

Ashley felt herself wrong-footed. 'Oh.'

'I saw the Facebook page you've organized about Mr Larcombe's funeral. I wondered if I could talk to you about it?' He paused as she still hadn't answered. 'If it's convenient, that is. I can always come back another time, if not.'

Ashley thought rapidly. She hadn't bargained on anyone finding her in person; she preferred to deal with them digitally and via the occasional phone call. It was disarming to have someone on her doorstep, especially an extremely attractive American. In her head she scanned the flat. It was too small not to keep tidy and, barring the takeaway pizza box that was evidence of her hasty supper, was fairly presentable. She got a grip. Why did she care what he thought anyway?

'I can go if you'd prefer?' he said, seeming to sense her hesitation.

Ashley remembered her manners. 'No please, come in.' She stepped back from the door. 'Go through.' She added with humour, 'You won't get lost.'

She followed him into the sitting room which served as kitchen and dining room too, picked up the remote and clicked off the television which had been burbling companionably in the background. She saw Eddie take in the open laptop, the coffee cup and empty plate.

'Aw jeez, you should have said you were working. I really don't want to disturb you if you're busy. Maybe I should go?'

Ashley rubbed a hand around the back of her neck to ease the cricks that had formed. She flashed him a smile. 'To be honest, I think I'm finished for the night. Would you like tea or maybe a coffee?'

'Tea would be good. Thank you.'

'Please, sit down.' Ashley nodded to the sofa. A pointless gesture, as it was the only seating. Eddie seemed much bigger when contained by this tiny flat. He unwound his stripy scarf and took off his leather jacket, revealing a cream pullover. She watched, amused, as he folded himself to fit onto the sofa.

'I was in the museum earlier. Talking to Noah. It's so great. I've got a real weakness for those places. Local museums that reflect the community they're in. And Berecombe's is a doozie. Your Noah is doing a wonderful job. He said he was off to a meeting this evening but would drop by later and that you probably wouldn't mind if I called by.'

Crossing to the kitchenette that stretched across one wall of the room, Ashley flicked on the kettle, trying to repress the suspicion that her cousin was playing matchmaker. Noah certainly seemed to hold the man in some esteem. That much was evident from their chance encounter in the café. 'Mint or builders'?'

'Excuse me?'

She turned and took pity on him. 'What sort of tea would you like? I've regular or mint.'

'Oh, regular's good. I'm developing a fondness for British tea. At home you get a bag on the side of a cup of hot water.' Eddie registered her shudder. 'I guess that's not the right way to make it?'

'Not quite.' She reached for the teapot and poured some hot water into it, swilling it around. 'I like the ritual of making it properly, although I have to confess to not always bothering if it's just for me.'

Eddie nodded. 'I'm the same with coffee. And rituals are important.'

She put the kettle back on to boil, emptied the water from the teapot and spooned in tea.

'I like the flat,' Eddie said.

Ashley turned. 'Thank you. It's a good colour scheme, isn't it? For somewhere by the sea. Blue and cream is soothing too. I think it's been used as a granny flat or a holiday let. Small but perfectly formed, and it's just right for me. For reasons best known to themselves, the owners didn't want the hassle of renting it out separately, so it got lumped in with Noah's bit. He thought it would be ideal for me and he's right.'

'You have the same surname. Noah is... what, your brother?'

'Cousin, but our fathers are twins, so we're probably more like brother and sister. Our families live near each other so we spent a lot of time together growing up before going to university. Noah is four years older, so disappeared off before me.' Ashley wrinkled her nose at the memory. 'I had some adjusting to do without him. We'd been at school together all the way through and he always looked out for me.'

'Still does, by the looks of things.'

Ashley laughed. 'Yes, I think he does. It didn't take him long to come up with the plan to help me escape from my parents. I was at a bit of a loose end at the time.' She paused, on the brink of saying something about the accident and then changed her mind. 'So here I am.' The kettle boiled and rescued her, so she busied herself with making the tea, finding some clean mugs and opening a packet of biscuits. Bringing the tray over to the coffee table, she put it down but decided against the sofa and sat on the floor. The sofa was barely big enough for one and, when seating two, had a nasty tendency to sag in the middle, causing its occupants to loll together in surprising intimacy.

'So, you teach at the university?' she asked, putting milk into the mugs.

'Yes. Came over August just gone. Coupla years' contract, but enjoying myself so much, I might stay. I lecture in American social history, specializing in post-World War Two.'

Ashley thought it sounded rather dry. 'Noah certainly knows you by reputation.'

'Probably more down to my hobby,' Eddie said ruefully. 'Since being here I've become fascinated by folk history, legends, stories people have passed down. I've developed quite a following doing talks for local groups.'

'Wow,' Ashley said, now more interested. 'There's

loads of folklore where I come from. Scratch the ground and up will come a legend, Dad always says.'

'Where's that?'

'I come from Ludlow in Shropshire. John Betjeman called it England's loveliest town. It's part of the Welsh Marches – castles dotted all down the English–Welsh border. We've got our own castle too.'

'Forgive me for doing the goofy Yank act, but I can never get over how there are so many castles in this country. So you come from a town with a real live castle?'

'Yes,' Ashley said, amused. 'Eleventh century. Mostly a ruin now, but enough of it left to see how it worked.' She poured the tea, remembering the strainer just in time. 'It's worth a visit. The town really is beautiful. Medieval with Georgian built on top. The castle is where Prince Arthur and Catherine of Aragon honeymooned – you know, Henry VIII's first wife. Always thought the poor woman didn't have much luck with husbands. Widowed by one brother, divorced by the other.'

Eddie accepted the mug she handed him, shaking his head. 'You guys. Always so blasé about your history.'

Ashley gave a wry smile. 'I suppose we've got a lot of it to be blasé about. Where are you from, Eddie? Clearly not Exeter.'

'I'm from Rockport, Massachusetts, on the east coast.

It's got its own history. Maybe that's why I like Berecombe so much. I like being close to the sea.'

'I suppose nowhere in the UK is far from the sea. An island nation, but I always think it's weird to say that.' Ashley put her mug down. 'And what brings you here tonight? You said you wanted to talk about Jimmy Larcombe's funeral?'

'Yes. Yes I did. It's a personal connection. You see, I'm sorta hoping he knew my grandfather.'

## Chapter Eight

Ashley blinked, taken aback. 'You think Jimmy Larcombe might have known your grandfather?' She frowned. 'How?'

Eddie nodded towards the teapot. 'Any more tea in there? This might take a while.'

As Ashley poured, Eddie began to explain. 'My grandfather was over here, in the war. World War Two, I mean.'

'In the UK?'

'In Berecombe.'

'Oh. In Berecombe itself?'

'He was part of Operation Overlord.' He saw her blank face. 'D-Day. The invasion of Europe by the Allies. Turning point of the war. Thanks,' he added, as she passed him his refilled mug. 'He was billeted in

Berecombe and went to Omaha from Weymouth. That's as much as we know.'

Ashley remembered now. Noah had talked about Omaha in the café. 'Can you ask him for more details, or would he rather not talk about it?'

'He passed a couple of years back.'

'I'm sorry.'

Eddie shrugged. 'He was an old man. He'd had what I believe you call over here, a good innings. Maybe he wasn't the easiest of men in his later years, but he was my grandpa, you know? He was good fun. When my mother finally got the guts to go through his things, we found a dog-tag.'

'A dog-tag?'

'The identity tag that all the GIs wore. It was in a tin box with, of all things, a load of old buttons.'

'And there was nothing else? No letters or medals.'

Eddie shook his head. 'Not a damn thing. Mom had no idea that he'd fought in the war, let alone took part in D-Day.'

'He never said anything? Talked about it?'

'Nope. Not a word. He had my mom when he was in his thirties. She was born in 63.' He grimaced. 'Other things going on closer to home to be discussed by then.'

'And you never knew he'd fought in the war?'

'He always clammed up whenever it was talked

about. We all sorta assumed he'd stayed home somehow. And Mom said it was the 60s. There was another war going on by then. More American kids drafted overseas to fight. Vietnam,' he added, as explanation. 'Mom got involved in the peace movement. Rebelling against her parents, she said. Except her pop backed her all the way. He said war was for old men to plan the deaths of the young.'

'That's some statement.' Ashley sipped her tea and, realizing it was over-stewed, put the mug down. 'Is that why you came over here? To find out about your grandfather?'

'Not exactly. At least not consciously. Things had got,' he paused, 'stale at home,' he added, carefully. 'Career not going anywhere.' His mouth twisted sourly. 'Got my heart broken by a girl I'd been in love with since forever. Mom got ill after Grandpa died. She got pregnant with me young and never had the chance to travel. She wanted me to get out in the world, experience something new. Told me to do it before it was too late. I was at a crossroads. Everything felt unsettled, you know what I mean?'

'I know exactly what you mean. So you took the lecturing post at Southwestern?'

'Yup. Came up at exactly the right time.'

'Perhaps it was meant to be.'

'Maybe.' He gave a short laugh and put his mug down with a decisive clunk. 'And so here I am, having traced my grandfather's steps this far, and I see your appeal on Berecombe town's Facebook page. A local man, another soldier who fought in France. It kind of got my hopes up.'

'What are you hoping to find out? I mean, it's unlikely any of Jimmy's contemporaries will still be alive.'

'No, I guess not.'

Eddie looked so deflated, it had Ashley wracking her brains for ways to help. He really wasn't at all the man she'd first thought from their encounter on the promenade. Still attractive, with those smooth American good looks, still with the air that he owned the world and could do whatever he liked with it. Now, however, she'd seen the sensitive underside, the one he covered with that slightly brash confidence, and she rather liked him for it. And he'd had his heart broken. Her own went out to him. 'The GIs!' she exclaimed.

'Yeah. Thought we'd covered that.' Eddie was bemused.

'The GIs who are coming over this spring. Did you know Noah is running a project to bring back the GIs who were stationed here?'

'No, I had no idea.' He shifted to the edge of the sofa in excitement. 'But that's so great!'

'You'll be able to ask them all sorts of things. If they want to talk about it,' Ashley added hastily. 'I think Noah is in touch with a regimental association. That might be able to help too.'

'I've got to give that a go.' He surged to his feet, towering above her on the floor. 'Aw, thanks so much, Ashley. It'll mean so much to Mom. It's her I'm doing this for.'

She began to get up, but having sat on the floor for so long, her left leg was stiff and her balance was off.

'Here, let me.' Eddie took her hands and helped her.

They stood for a second hand in hand, facing one another. Ashley could feel heat coming off him, and a sudden, incomprehensible desire rippled through her. She began to move away; complications of that sort were definitely not needed at the moment. Still wobbly, she caught her foot on the edge of the rug.

'Hey,' he said, catching her and holding her against him. 'Careful.'

She gazed up at him. At the strong chin and jawline, at the dimple in his right cheek that was somehow incredibly erotic and begging to be kissed, at the kindness and humour in his hazel eyes. His arms were a strong band around her back, wool-covered steel, and she didn't want to leave his hold. She found herself pressed against his thighs and they were hard too. Another pulse of longing exploded.

Eddie shifted closer, his mouth lowered fractionally. 'Ashley?'

The moment was interrupted by someone hammering on the door. The letterbox rattled open and Noah yelled through, 'Ash, you in there? Left any pizza for me?'

## Chapter Nine

Ashley stepped back, wondering if it was a look of regret on Eddie's face or if she had imagined it. 'I'd better get the door,' she said lamely. She moved into the hall, every inch of her yearning to be back in his arms. What the hell was happening to her? She simply couldn't fall for someone she barely knew.

Noah burst into the flat, his energy making the space even smaller. 'Oh, hi Eddie. Good, you're still here.'

'I am, but I'd better go.' Eddie glanced at his watch. 'Jeez,' he said, his brows shooting up. 'I really need to go. Hadn't realized the time.'

'You've missed the last train,' Noah pointed out. 'Look, why don't you stay over? Kip at my place.'

'You sure?'

'Wouldn't suggest it if I didn't mean it.' Noah rubbed

his hands together. 'Ash, have you any pizza left or have you been a greedy guts and eaten the lot?'

'There are two slices left. I was saving them for tomorrow.'

'Saving them?' Noah said incredulously. *'Saving* them? You're such a girl sometimes. Let me at them. I'm starving.'

Ashley laughed. 'In the box on the cupboard over there. Would you like me to heat them up?'

'Nah. I'll eat them cold. Beer?'

'In the fridge.'

'Fantastic. Seeing as you're staying, can I interest you in a beer, Eddie?'

Eddie sent a questioning, half-apologetic glance Ashley's way. She shrugged and smiled. 'Sure,' he said. 'A beer sounds great, especially a cold one.'

Noah, his head in the fridge, said, 'Don't tell me you're one of those Americans who hasn't taken a liking to our beer?'

Eddie sat back on the sofa and grinned. 'You mean the warm frothy kind with names like Old Badger's Nose?' He winked conspiratorially at Ashley.

'Those are the ones.' Noah emerged from the fridge with three bottles. 'I can see I'm going to have to spend some time on your education.' He took the caps off and handed one to Eddie.

This was too much for Ashley. 'Oh Noah, at least have the decency to use a glass!'

'Sorry, coz.' Noah opened a cupboard and poured her beer into a glass. He slumped down on the floor with his bottle, the pizza box open on his knee.

Ashley perched on the very edge of the sofa, remembering its sagginess. She wasn't sure she wanted to be pressed against any part of Eddie at the moment. At least not just yet. Their encounter a few minutes ago had been disturbing and had sent her senses out of control. And she didn't like being out of control. Unsettled, she glared at Noah.

'What?' he said, waving his pizza slice around, one huge bite already taken.

'You. You're such a boy sometimes.'

'Yup,' he said, unabashed. 'What have you two been up to, then?'

Ashley turned to Eddie. 'Would you like to tell him, or shall I?'

Eddie gestured with his beer bottle. 'Happy for you to. Go ahead.'

'Ho ho,' Noah said, lasciviously. 'What *have* you two been up to?'

Ashley raised an eyebrow, hoping she wasn't blushing. 'What did I say? Such a boy.' She outlined the conversation she and Eddie had had. 'So, we thought it might be an idea for Eddie to talk to the GIs who come over, if any manage to,' she finished.

'Can't see why not.' Noah closed the pizza box and wiped his hands on a paper serviette. 'And you really had no idea your grandfather fought on Omaha?'

'None whatsoever. He never talked about it. Never talked about the war, period.'

'Astonishing.' Noah screwed the serviette up and shoved it into the box. 'Well, there's a reasonable chance of one of the veterans knowing him. I believe there was only one battalion billeted in Berecombe, but that was made up of several companies, probably amounting to about a thousand men in total. They would have come over on the boat together and then travelled down from Liverpool. They arrived in winter, which even on the south coast can be pretty damp and miserable.' He shook his head. 'Makes you wonder what they made of it all. Must have been the most foreign place any of them had ever been. And they were so young.'

'Did they know what they were here for?' Ashley asked.

'I expect they had a pretty good idea. The finer details were kept from them until they needed to know. The locals knew nothing, of course. And if they did know, they said nothing. You couldn't. "Careless talk costs lives" was the saying. It was a crucial time in the war and no one wanted to jeopardize anything.'

'So brave,' Ashley murmured. 'I mean, they came over, most of them only in their twenties.'

'Younger,' Noah put in. 'The average age of the men who went from Berecombe was nineteen and a half.'

'Away from their homes for the first time. Fighting a foreign war. Not knowing what to expect.' She turned to Eddie. 'You must be very proud of your grandfather.'

He took a slug of beer. 'Certainly am.' He sat up and rolled the beer bottle between his hands. 'I can't get over how he had a whole life before he married, had children, a career. A whole life none of us knew anything about.'

'Perhaps it was too painful to talk about?' Ashley suggested.

'Or maybe,' Noah added, 'it was one part of his life. One segment. By the time he had your mum he'd moved on, become a different person, wanted a different life. He'd lived through a cataclysmic event, one that must have challenged him to the core. Maybe he wanted a new life that had nothing to do with the war. It might even have been a relief for him.' He flicked a glance at Ashley.

'That I can relate to,' she said.

Eddie, watching the exchange curiously, drained his bottle. 'It's late,' he said. 'This conversation's getting heavy. More beer, or do we turn in?'

Ashley straightened. 'I can answer that. If you want more beer, you'll have to go up to Noah's. I don't have any more here. And, if you don't mind me being a girl again, one beer is enough for me tonight. I'm rather tired.'

'We hear you, coz.' Noah pulled himself wearily to his feet. 'I have more beer upstairs, Eddie, or we can sort you out a bed. It's a sofa-bed but not uncomfortable.' He kissed Ashley on the top of the head. 'Sweet dreams. We'll leave you in peace.'

She saw them to the door, which was faintly ridiculous, as it was Noah's house and he knew the way. 'Good night,' she said, watching them head off for the main entrance.

Eddie turned back just before he disappeared from view. 'Good night, Ashley,' he said softly. 'Sleep well.'

She closed the door and leaned on it. *Fat chance,* she thought. Closing her eyes, her vison was full of his searching hazel eyes, the sardonic curve of his upper lip. Her skin still throbbed from the feel of his arms. 'Get a grip, woman,' she scolded herself. 'You don't even know him!'

## Chapter Ten

Ashley had no time to linger on the sensual delights of Eddie McQueen as, early the next morning, she was woken by her phone vibrating. It was Keeley Sharma from the local paper wanting to interview her for a piece about Jimmy Larcombe and asking if tomorrow afternoon was convenient. Ashley thought quickly. She had no great desire to be interviewed; in her experience journalists always wanted to put their own spin on the story, even at the local rag level. She'd never quite forgiven a former schoolfriend who had turned in a piece on her accident, hinting blame could be placed on both drivers. It had ignited an unwelcome series of articles and letters to the local paper which had lasted for some time and had come when Ashley was feeling at her lowest.

'Well, Keeley. If you want anything out of me, I'll turn it to my advantage,' she murmured. 'Tomorrow's fine,' she said into the phone, 'but can I ask a favour? Have you a room big enough for a meeting?'

———

Ashley splashed out on a cab. The following day, Alf the taxi driver picked her up at two sharp. *The Berecombe News* offices were in a business park on the outskirts of town and impossible to get to by bus. Greeted by an effervescent Keeley in a crowded reception, she was gratified to see everyone she'd invited had made it. The Reverend Erica Lesley, Andrea, the manager from Fir Tree Hall, Biddy, and Petra from the café were all there. Elvis, smart in a waterproof quilted jacket, stood to attention at Biddy's knees.

After they had greeted one another, Keeley led them all into a conference room. A table dominated the space and picture windows flooded the room with light. A tray of coffee stood waiting. 'I thought this would be the best space for us all,' she said. 'We all share one big open-plan office and it's not conducive to meetings. Gets far too noisy. Come and sit down, enjoy the view and grab yourselves a coffee. Just give me a minute, will you? I need to get my gear together.'

Ashley sat in the chair Keeley pulled out for her and accepted the mug of coffee Andrea had poured. She couldn't believe her luck in getting everyone here at such short notice. Torn between the view of the rolling valley leading down to the town and the sea, or observing their host, she decided on the latter. She wished she'd thought to bring her camera along but it seemed a bit coals to Newcastle and had left it at home. Keeley had an arresting face: long straight black hair framed an olive-complexioned oval face and enormous brown eyes. She watched as the journalist gathered her pen and notebook, clicked on the handheld recorder which looked remarkably similar to the one Noah used, and looked up.

'What?'

Ashley shook herself. 'Sorry, you caught me staring. How rude. I take photographs. I was just thinking you'd make a marvellous subject. You've got a very interesting face.'

'Who, me?' Keeley laughed, showing even white teeth, vivid against her cherry-red lipstick.

Ashley was embarrassed. 'It was just something Noah was saying. About me taking photographs around the town. Of the people and landmarks.'

'That's Noah who is in charge of the museum now, isn't it? Have to say, his arrival last autumn caused a bit of a sensation here. We're used to people retiring to

Berecombe, not handsome, young gallants riding into town, all guns blazing.'

'My cousin's a bit like that,' Ashley admitted. 'His enthusiasm for things can get the better of him.'

'Oh, don't apologize. It's a breath of fresh air. We need someone to shake things up every now and again. He's your cousin then, not husband?'

*Yet another Noah conquest,* Ashley thought, amused. They were mounting up. 'Definitely not my husband.' She gave a quick shudder. 'The very thought exhausts me. He can be quite hard to keep up with when he gets going.'

'How very intriguing.' Keeley pulled a suggestive face.

'I'll pass on your compliments.'

Keeley laughed again. She seemed the laughing sort and Ashley warmed to her. 'Please do. And tell him next time I'll pop by the museum and interview him in person, rather than over the telephone. And if you ever feel the need to photograph me, give me a call. Now, shall we start the meeting? I understand you wanted everyone here to rally the troops, so to speak?'

Ashley took in a deep breath. 'Yes. I know it was rather cheeky of me but, with time pressing, I thought it would be a chance to get together and see what we could all bring to Jimmy's funeral and wake.'

'What a marvellous idea,' Andrea said, beaming. She was a large, comfortably serene woman in her fifties. 'I'm thrilled! Do you know, when I contacted the paper initially, I rather hoped some publicity might be generated, but I'm afraid I just didn't have the time to do anything more. Jimmy was such a special resident and we were all so terribly fond of him. I hated the thought that it might just be me and the vicar at the funeral. As it so often is when our residents reach such a grand old age.' She gave Erica a moist-eyed look and the vicar patted her hand.

'Jimmy made me executor of his will,' Erica explained. 'A somewhat unorthodox request, but he was always such a keen and supportive member of my church that I didn't dream of hesitating. I've been in touch with his solicitors and they were in agreement that it was an excellent idea to try to encourage as many people as possible to give Jimmy this fantastic send-off. I've got his list of hymns and readings – Jimmy had it all sorted – and we'll encourage anyone who is happy to say a few words to do so.'

'He was such a larger-than-life character,' Andrea added. 'He would have loved all this fuss. Besides, this year of all years, I think we need to remember our wartime heroes.'

'Andrea, do you think you could put together a board

with some photos?' Ashley asked. 'Perhaps we could put it up at the wake?'

'I'd be happy to. I'll sort through a few as soon as I get back. I know there's a lovely one of Jimmy dressed as Father Christmas. He used to do it for the local primary school until he was well into his eighties.' She peered into her handbag. 'Actually, I've got one of him here. Would you like to see? I thought it might help the social media campaign. Think it must have been taken some time in the 50s.'

Ashley took the black and white photograph with trembling fingers. Jimmy had obviously splashed out on a studio session, as it had the name of the professional photographer in one corner. He was sitting in a stiff-backed chair, his hands grasping the arms. His posture was rigid, formal and slightly nervous. She followed the line of his double-breasted jacket to the sharp-collared shirt and dark tie, and then gasped as she saw his face. 'He had a scar!'

'Oh yes,' Andrea said, unperturbed. 'Think he got it in the war but he never talked about it. Do you know, I never thought of his scar. Once you got to know Jimmy, it was the last thing you noticed about him. The first was his eyes. Naughty. Brimming over with mischievousness and life. He regularly had the ladies of the home squabbling over his affections.'

Ashley examined the photograph more closely, thinking hard. No one had ever mentioned a scar and yet you could hardly miss it. Her own was insignificant by comparison. It trailed a wide, jagged path down the man's face from the corner of his right eye, skirting the nose and the corner of the mouth and over his chin. Ashley could see it disappearing under the closely buttoned shirt collar. Goodness knows where it ended. From her limited knowledge gained from the scar clinic she'd attended, she guessed it to be from a burn. The skin was too widely affected and raised and puckered to be anything else. Her hand flew to her throat. Poor Jimmy. Having to face life with something so dramatic and impossible to conceal. She knew he'd had a job with the council. A fairly anonymous pen-pushing post in an office, but one that kept him away from the general public. He would have been in a team of people he knew well, who knew him well and accepted him – and his scar. He wouldn't have had to constantly explain himself or go into the story of how he became so mutilated. Ashley understood completely. Jimmy hadn't hidden himself away exactly, simply surrounded himself with the same people day in, day out, so that they had eventually accepted him for what he was. A man with a scar, not a walking disfigurement. And, from what she'd heard about the man, he'd not let it stand in his way.

Andrea's words echoed: 'It was the last thing you noticed about Jimmy.' There was a lesson there. For her.

She became aware that the others were staring at her and she swallowed the sudden tears. 'Could we also put out a book for people to fill in their memories?' she said croakily, forcing herself to focus. 'Petra, is Millie okay with us taking over the café for the morning?'

'Yes, she's cool with it.' Petra nodded, the red and white spotted bow in her hair bobbing. 'I rang her and we talked through the menu. We'll keep it simple, as we don't know how many people there'll be. A selection of sandwiches and cakes and mini scones with clotted cream and jam.'

'Cream first, I hope, the Devon way,' Biddy butted in.

Andrea grimaced comically. 'Have to confess to being more of a jam-then-cream kind of girl.' She giggled. 'That way you can pile more cream on.'

'Well you'd best move to Cornwall then.' Biddy glared. 'That's how they insist on doing it over the border.'

'Nothing gets the West Country riled up more than the correct way to dress a scone,' Keeley whispered to Ashley, with a grin.

'Okaaay,' Ashley said, nonplussed. As Biddy opened her mouth to speak again, she said quickly, 'Biddy, could

I ask you and the Women's Institute a huge favour? Could you serve the refreshments? It would be such a help.'

'We'd be honoured. We can help with making the food too.'

'Thanks Biddy,' Petra added. 'That takes a load off. Ashley, do you want me to take down the bunting I'd planned for the seventy-fifth anniversary? Not everyone will think it's fitting for a funeral.'

'Actually, could I answer that?' Erica leaned forward. 'I see Jimmy's funeral service and wake as the celebration of a long life lived well. I think the bunting should stay.'

'Jimmy always loved a party,' Andrea added. 'And, as he was in the war, the colour scheme suits.'

'Then I'll leave it up,' Petra said, looking relieved. 'There's quite a lot of it and I put it up for the commemorations this year. It'll save me a job, not having to take it down.'

'I think Jimmy would thoroughly approve,' Erica said.

'The more I hear about Jimmy Larcombe,' Ashley said, with a smile, 'the more I like the sound of him.'

'And he would have loved you,' Andrea said gleefully. 'He always had an eye for the ladies. Kept us all on our toes at the Hall, that's for certain. One of his favourite things to do was challenge the other residents to wheelchair races around the grounds. We were forever rescuing waifs and strays from the soft ground by the pond. Jimmy used to tell them it was a shortcut and they'd get their wheels stuck. Meantime, he was back at the Hall claiming victory. And his jokes!' Andrea rolled her eyes. 'They were dreadful, truly dreadful, but he kept them coming.' She wiped a tear away from the corner of her eye. 'How I wish he was here to tell us one now.'

Erica reached over and patted her hand again. 'I'm going to have to add that to my eulogy.'

'He sounds wonderful and I really wish I'd met him,' Ashley said, feeling the affection the women had for Jimmy; it was almost palpable.

'This is a marvellous thing you're doing,' Erica said. 'Bless you. It needed one person to kick us all into gear.'

'You know,' Keeley interrupted, 'it strikes me that *this* is the story. Not so much Jimmy Larcombe's life and funeral but the community coming together like this. Making an event like this happen.'

'I think we have Ashley to thank for that,' Petra said.

'But I couldn't do it without all of you. Without Keeley to publicize it, you to do the catering, Andrea telling us what Jimmy was like and Erica to lead the service.'

'Berecombe may have its faults,' Biddy put in stoutly,

'but the one thing we're really good at is coming together as a community.'

Ashley remembered Noah saying something similar. 'Absolutely,' she said and smiled at Biddy, who humphed a bit and fussed with Elvis.

'Well, I suppose I ought to do my interview now,' Keeley said. 'But I think I have my story. Ashley, have you any idea how many you'll get coming? Have these sorts of appeals proved successful before?'

Ashley shook her head. 'I simply don't know. I've had a hundred or so emails but most of those were from people sending their best wishes but not able to come. Or spam.' Screwing up her face, she added, 'Or military men tragically widowed and looking for a special friendship.' She leaned forward suddenly. 'What I'd really like to achieve is to make contact with someone who actually knew him. A relative or friend. That would make it all more meaningful.' She put her coffee mug on the table, staring at it and wondering how she had got so involved in an elderly man's funeral. But Jimmy Larcombe was coming to mean something to her. A man who had lived such a life deserved a good send-off.

'You know, what might help is the local news channel.' Keeley tapped her pen against her teeth. 'It's just the feel-good story they'd be after on regional news. I have some contacts I could put you in touch with, if you like.'

'Oh, that's a fabulous idea,' Petra said. 'You should so do that!'

'I don't know,' Ashley said, alarmed. 'Being in the local paper is one thing, appearing on television is a whole other ballgame. I don't think I could do that.'

'Why, because you're physically challenged?' Keeley nodded to the stick. 'There's a story I'd love to write. Why you've chosen to come to Berecombe.'

'I'm not, I just happen to walk with a stick. And there's no story there at all. I want this to be about Jimmy Larcombe, not me,' Ashley replied firmly, her heart sinking. Was this going to be Keeley's angle? She hoped not.

'In which case, television's the way to go. They'd lap you up on *Focus Southwest* and there would always be the chance it would go national. Think of the people you could reach that way. The ones who aren't on social media. The ones who watch their local news magazine programme without fail every teatime.'

'Young Keeley here has got a point,' Biddy said. 'Not everyone, especially folk of a certain vintage, are as clued up with computers as I am. Take Beryl, for instance. Wouldn't know her dongle from a hard drive.'

'And quite often people watch local news on catch-up, especially if they've moved away from the area,' Keeley added, pressing her point home.

It was a convincing argument, but it still had Ashley coming out in a cold sweat at the thought of appearing on TV. 'Let me think about it,' she said slowly.

'Well, don't think about it for too long. The funeral's soon, isn't it?' Keeley raised one perfectly groomed eyebrow. 'Need to get a shift on. Tell you what, I'll pass the story on to my contact and you can make the decision if she gets in touch with you. If there's a lot of other news going on, it might not make the cut anyway.' She stood up abruptly. 'And now I have to get this written up. It'll be in this week's edition. We've cleared some space. I'll send Andy through to take a few snaps of you all. No point me hanging about.'

Ashley didn't think Keeley hung about with anything. She rose too. 'No. Absolutely not.'

'My TV contact can get you on the same number?'

'Yes.' Ashley sat down again, feeling a little dazed.

'Good. Did you come by car? No? Reception will ring for a taxi when you're ready. Give your gorgeous cousin a kiss from me.' And, with that, Keeley strode out.

The group of women chattered and fussed with their hair in readiness for the photographer, who was almost as cursory as Keeley, and before she knew it, Ashley was getting back into a taxi, coincidentally driven by the same man.

'Useful afternoon then, my lovely?' Alf asked.

'Do you know, I have absolutely no idea.' Ashley sat back against the head-rest feeling ever so slightly mugged off. She really hoped Keeley would go nowhere near Noah. He wouldn't stand a chance.

## Chapter Eleven

'Well, it's absolutely fabulous that you've got a TV interview,' Noah said, his eyes not leaving his computer screen. 'Should move the publicity campaign on a pace, shouldn't it?'

They were ensconced in his eyrie of an office in the museum. The good weather had deserted Berecombe and a chill wind blew sand off the beach onto the promenade. Ashley watched as a few hardy dog walkers combated the elements. One had a tiny Yorkshire terrier who was refusing to budge in the face of the gale, so its owner picked it up and half jogged to the shelter of the high street, head bowed down.

'It should,' she answered slowly.

Noah evidently heard the note of uncertainty in her voice and swung round. 'But what?'

Ever since Ashley had heard from the *Focus Southwest* programme she'd been trying to find excuses not to do it. She freely admitted to herself that it was cowardly. 'I—' she began and then looked down and scuffed her feet.

'Ash. What's wrong?'

She looked at him, her face screwed up in embarrassment.

'You know this lack of confidence thing is all in your head.'

'Well, duh!'

'You're more than capable of doing this interview.' He skidded his chair along the floor and took her hands in his. 'You're more than capable of doing anything. It's time to get your life going again, Ash.'

'I know, but it's all getting a bit out of hand, Noah. I had another hundred and fifty emails to wade through this morning. I'm really worried about what I've started. What happens if thousands turn up at Jimmy's funeral?'

'Don't be daft,' Noah said robustly. 'That's hardly likely to happen.'

'Not if I don't do the telly. But it might escalate out of all proportion if I do. I want Jimmy to have a decent send-off, not a mob riot.'

Noah peered searchingly into his cousin's eyes. 'Except that's not the real reason you're reluctant, is it, darling coz?'

Ashley blew her fringe out of her eyes. 'Okay,' she admitted. 'I suppose anyone would feel nervous about being interviewed on TV, and concerns about Jimmy's funeral being overrun aside, what I'm really worried about is—'

'What?'

'My scar.'

Noah reared back. 'Your scar?' he said incredulously. 'You can hardly see it.'

'But it's there.' Ashley put a self-conscious hand to her hair and flicked it over her ear. 'I know it's there. It's why I've kept my hair long. Straight after the accident Mum wanted me to have it all cut off. Said it would be far more practical if short. Easier to wash. But I insisted I kept it long, even though I knew she was right, if I'm honest.'

'And *you* were right. It covers what's left of your scar beautifully. Besides,' Noah put a coquettish hand through his own thick mop of dark hair. 'Isn't it our family trademark? I believe we Lyddens have been complimented many times on our luscious brown locks.'

She managed a laugh. 'True.'

'Let me have a look. I really don't think it's as bad as you think.'

She turned her right side to him and he gently lifted the hair away from her face. The scar, running from

Ashley's temple to behind her ear, had faded to a silvery pink thin line. Her hair, which had had to be partially shaved, was growing back over it, the short layers blending into the longer ones.

'It's barely noticeable, Ash,' Noah said softly. 'The plastic surgeon did a great job.'

'Truth?' She reverted to the language of their childhood.

'Truth. Just have one of those Veronica Lake hairdos and hide one eye.'

'Who?'

'1940s film star, famous for her peek-a-boo hairstyle. Gorgeous.' He grinned. 'I've been in meetings with the Regent Theatre trying to decide what films to put on as part of the film festival. Veronica Lake was the hottie of the time and she had one lock of hair that fell over one eye. Very alluring. Mike Love and I were quite taken.'

'Mike Love? The theatre director?' Ashley's eyes widened.

Noah allowed himself to look smug. 'I'm moving in the highest circles these days, don't you know.'

'Get you,' she said.

'He's patron of the theatre. Local boy made good. Still got a house in the town.'

'And drop-dead gorgeous.'

'Well, I find him so.'

They laughed.

'Okay,' Ashley said. 'I'll agree to do the interview, peek-a-whatsit hairstyle notwithstanding, but I have one other problem.'

'What's that, oh coz divine?'

'The studios are in Plymouth. How the hell am I supposed to get there?'

'Get where?' said a well-modulated American voice from the doorway.

Noah turned to Ashley and raised one dark brow impishly. 'I do believeth your knight in shining armour hath arriveth!'

## Chapter Twelve

'This is amazingly good of you,' Ashley said, two days later, as she glanced across the car to Eddie. 'I mean, driving all the way into Berecombe and then back the way you came in order to pick up the Plymouth road.' He seemed slightly more relaxed now they were out of Berecombe, on the main road and heading west.

He gave a tight grin. 'This is the way I came so I know the route. And I'm getting more used to driving on the left now.'

'You mean the right side of the road, don't you?' Ashley couldn't resist.

'Aw, jeez. I'm having enough trouble as it is. Don't confuse me any further.' He crunched a gear. 'And why don't you guys drive automatic? I hate driving stick.'

She watched as he cupped the gear knob in his

strong-looking hand and thrust it into fourth. His mouth was compressed into a thin line of concentration and he hadn't once looked away from the road ahead. She took pity on him. 'Have you driven in the UK much?'

'Only a few times. Chickened out most of the time and took the train. Or the bus. I like the view from the top deck. But I figured I had to do more driving. Public transport won't get me everywhere.'

'Then you're very brave. Braver than me. I haven't driven since the— Well, I haven't driven for ages. I'm not even a very good passenger nowadays.' She tried not to flinch as a car overtook them. It had been difficult and, sometimes, impossible to get into a car in the early days following her recovery. She still refused to sit in a car when it was parked up.

Eddie risked a quick look across. 'You don't seem *too* nervous.'

Ashley flashed a grin back. 'Must be your driving.'

'Or preoccupation about the interview?'

'Or that.' She laughed. 'I'm very nervous about that.'

'You'll be fine,' he said, reassuringly. 'Just be yourself.'

'I will. If I can decide who that is.'

'Someday you need to tell me about all this. Why you don't drive. Why you're as jumpy as a cat sometimes.'

'Maybe.'

'But not while I'm driving, huh? I need to concentrate. Maybe it'll be easier when we hit the freeway.'

'I don't think we'll be on the M5 much but I think the A38 is a dual carriageway. Or nearly as good as.' She stopped talking as the sat-nav cut in and gave them complicated directions. 'She's very stern, isn't she?'

Eddie laughed. 'I call her Biddy Two. Noah filled me in about her. Wouldn't dare to disobey the redoubtable Biddy. Did you catch any of that?'

'Not a thing. But, if I remember the map correctly, just head onto the M5 slip road and follow the signs south.'

'Just as well you're here.'

'I may be a nervous passenger but I have a photographic memory for maps. Noah says it's extremely unfeminine of me. He, of course, gets lost all the time. Permanently late, is my cousin.'

'Nothing unfeminine about you, Ashley.'

'Well, thank you.' She glowed inwardly at the compliment. He was proving very easy company. When he had come across them in the museum office and Noah had explained her problem, Eddie had immediately offered to drive her to the *Focus Southwest* studios. He'd batted off her suggestion that she could easily get a train, saying she'd have to mess about with taxis on top of the train from Axminster. 'We'll make a day of it,' he'd said.

'It'll be fun.' And now, as he steered the VW onto the slip road and headed Plymouth-bound, she began to relax ever so slightly too. Despite his protestations, he seemed a competent driver. She flicked a lock of hair over her face, conscious that her scarred side was next to him.

'And one day,' he said quietly, 'maybe you'll tell me how you got that.'

Ashley looked down at her suddenly clenched hands and didn't answer.

Inevitably, despite Biddy Two's help, they took a wrong turn and got lost. Ashley spotted a street name she remembered, Eddie took a sharp right and they ended up coming to the studios from the wrong end.

'Well, despite everything, I got you here,' he said. 'Now, if I can only find somewhere to park. You sure don't like generously sized parking lots over here, do you?'

Ashley had to agree. The car park was rammed. Just as she feared she'd be late, she spotted a space and Eddie squeezed the car in. 'Come on,' he said, glancing at his watch. 'We'll have to hurry.'

A runner named Izzy led them along to a musty-smelling green room where they were offered tea or coffee. 'Or there's wine over there if you need to, like, steady your nerves. Chloe will be along in a mo. We'll record the interview now and show it later in the main prog after the national news. Unless, of course, something comes up that makes your piece drop off.' Izzy pursed her lips and shook her head. 'Don't worry though, that literally hardly ever happens. You'll only be about an hour and then you can, like, get home to watch yourself.' She beamed and left them to it.

Eddie had just poured himself a coffee when a slim, well-preserved woman strode into the room. She was wearing a skirt suit in bright turquoise and matching stilettoes. Running up to Ashley on trippy little toes, she took her hands and exclaimed, 'You must be Ashley. How absolutely darling to meet you. I'm Chloe Deverell but you've probably recognized me. I can't wait to hear your story. You're from Berecombe, aren't you?' Without waiting for an answer she went on, 'I covered a story there last year. All about the town getting Free Trade status, bless it. I remember interviewing a rather yummy man.' She wrinkled her perfect snub nose. 'Jed Henville... or something? He was lush, darling.' She gave a trill laugh. 'Probably shouldn't say things like that, but it makes the job a teensy bit more bearable.' Making a dramatic swoop around, she fixed her eyes on Eddie. Batting her tawny-coloured lashes, she asked, 'And who is *this*?'

'Eddie McQueen.' He stepped forward and shook Chloe's hand. 'How great to meet you. I'm not really involved in the project, just drove Ashley here and have come to support.'

'How marvellous of you. And may I say what a delicious accent. East coast?'

'Yup.'

Chloe's flirting went into overdrive. 'Are you sure you don't want to join in on the interview? The camera would love you.' She swept him with a look from toes to head in a manner that made her real meaning crystal clear.

Eddie laughed. 'It's not my gig. The Jimmy Larcombe project is all Ashley's.'

Chloe pouted. 'Totes shame.' Turning reluctantly back to Ashley, she added, 'Good to see you took our advice on what to wear.' She rolled her eyes. 'So many don't. Stripes dance around on the screen and can be terribly distracting. And no one could possibly say that pale-blue top is anything but ordinary. The viewers can concentrate on your message. Come along, this way, we'll get you into make-up so you don't look quite so green about the gills, and then we'll get started. Won't take long. Oh, and lose the stick.'

Ashley stared at Eddie. 'Help,' she whispered. 'The woman's a monster.'

'You'll be fine,' he mouthed, obviously trying not to laugh. 'Good luck.'

## Chapter Thirteen

She was back in the green room before she knew it. Despite Ashley's misgivings, Chloe had been a professional interviewer. The main points had been covered and at the end, Chloe turned to the camera and appealed directly to the viewers. 'So,' she said, simpering, head on one side. 'If you knew Mr Larcombe, or if you're a relative, I implore you to get in touch, either with Ashley here or via us at the studios. Let's make Jimmy Larcombe's funeral one fit for the hero he truly was.' Then she became engrossed in her notes and said nothing more to Ashley. It was up to a frazzled-looking Izzy to lead her back to the claustrophobic green room, where Eddie was waiting.

Ashley collapsed onto the sofa and eyed the wine

covetously. It was still only eleven-thirty, though. Far too early for alcohol.

'How did it go?' Eddie asked. 'Looked A-okay from where I was sitting.'

Ashley blew out a breath, relieved it was all over. 'I'm not sure. Well, I think I said most of what I wanted to say.' She glanced at the TV monitor high up on one wall. It was now showing a heated discussion between Chloe and the floor manager. 'Who knows, though? They might edit me to make me look stupid. They might cut me out altogether.'

'They might, but hey – you can only do what you can do.'

'Very true.'

'Can I get you a drink?'

'Do you know, now it's all over, I'd rather just go. This place is stifling.'

'Sure. Let's hit the road and grab some lunch.'

---

They stopped in Sidmouth, at a tiny pub just off the seafront. It had bleached wooden floors, a roaring open fire and a simple menu. They found a table in the Regency bay and squeezed in, close together, onto the window seat. Outside, against a gull-grey sky, shoppers hurried past, wrapped up in the face of a March sleet storm.

'I'm starved,' Eddie announced, picking up the menu. 'Think I'll have the crab. I love me some seafood. What can I get you to drink?'

Ashley was frozen. 'Hot chocolate, if they do it. A latte if not. And soup for lunch, please.' She peered into the dark interior of the pub. 'Looks like you order at the bar.' As Eddie sauntered off to order, she took time to admire him. She'd been so preoccupied by the interview, she hadn't properly looked at him all morning. Now she watched as he leaned against the bar and chatted to the barmaid. He'd taken off his leather jacket to reveal a navy sleeveless sweater over a grandad shirt and tweed trousers. Very preppy. Very American somehow. She was reminded of Harrison Ford in the very first Indiana Jones movie and smiled; she'd always fancied Indiana Jones more when he was in professor mode. She bit down a grin as she noticed the barmaid checking him out as he made his way back to their table. Eddie McQueen, even without the easy charm, was a very attractive man.

He unwound his scarf and draped it over the back of a chair, on top of his jacket. 'What's making you laugh?'

'Oh, nothing. How did you find this place?'

'One of the guys in the department mentioned it. Said

the food was good.' He sat back down, eased a kink out of his neck and grimaced. 'Breaks the journey back too.'

'Thank you for driving me. I really appreciate it. By the time I'd got taxis, it would have used up all of the day. And it's so cold today, it would have been miserable on public transport.'

'It's no trouble, Ashley,' he said softly. He gave her his trademark smile, the groove in his cheek deepening, and then sat back on the window seat, resting his arm along the top.

'But it was,' Ashley insisted, only too aware of his well-muscled arm warm on her back. 'It's taken a lot of your time and it's meant you had to drive. And I can tell you don't find it easy driving on the left.'

'I wouldn't have offered if I hadn't wanted to. And, hey, it's great to spend time with you.' He slipped a lock of her hair through his fingers, concentrating on it with narrowed eyes. His touch made her nerves sing. 'I had no lectures today. And the driving, well, it just takes more focus, you know. The roads over here are narrower, more congested.' He shook his head ruefully, his hair flopping over his forehead. It made him look younger. 'And your roundabouts. I really have to stop and figure those little critters out. Most of our roads are built on a grid system with intersections.'

'Then lunch is on me. As a thank-you.'

He grinned at her, eyes twinkling with humour. 'Accepted with pleasure. On one condition.'

'What's that?'

'That I take you out for dinner to pay you back.'

Ashley traced an indentation in the wooden tabletop, suddenly shy. She liked this man. It was madness – she hardly knew him. She fancied him rotten, of course, but acknowledged that was simply a reaction to his very considerable physical charms. Much more than a hormonal response, she really liked him, being in his company, his humour, his intellect. His kindness. And she had no idea how he felt about her.

'Deal?'

'Deal,' she answered, trying not to blush as she gazed back at him and their eyes met. The moment was heated up by Snow Patrol bursting out of the speaker. Ashley was suddenly very aware that, as in the words of the song, she'd like to lie with Eddie very much. She could happily forget the world when with him. And then the barmaid brought their drinks and Ashley crashed back down into reality and her hot chocolate. Funny. She didn't feel like it now. Eddie's proximity had warmed her up.

Their food followed. Eddie admired his crab served in its shell and accompanied by chunky granary bread and thick wedges of lemon. As he squeezed the lemon's juice out, he asked casually, 'You walked without your stick back there in the studios. Do you not need it all the time?'

Ashley deliberated. She longed to be considered as more than someone who had problems walking but acknowledged it was an obvious question. 'On flat surfaces and when I'm not tired, no. Stairs, cobbles, when it's the end of a long day and I'm tired, then yes. I'm trying not to use it as often but it's a crutch.' She laughed. 'Quite literally.' She glanced at her curried parsnip soup which had arrived served in a cottage loaf. 'Do you think I'm supposed to eat the bread too?'

'Don't see why not.' As she spooned up the first mouthful, he asked, 'Good?'

'Delicious. I can feel it warming me right down to my cockles.'

'Okay. I have no idea what you mean but I'll go with it.' There was a pause while they ate and then he added, 'Noah mentioned you'd been in an accident.'

Ashley cursed her cousin silently. He had no right to tell strangers details of her private history. But then, Eddie didn't seem like a stranger. Oddly, he never had. When he'd called round at the flat they'd talked with a quick and easy intimacy. It was peculiar. She felt she'd known him for forever. And it had been much easier telling Biddy about what had happened than she'd feared. It was only natural, she supposed, that people would be curious. Perhaps this defence against the world and all its questions should stop. People wanted to know. She only had to answer.

'I had a car accident.'

'Jeez. What happened?' Eddie had cut up his food and had put his knife down, ready to eat with his fork. He paused, all attention, the fork halfway to his mouth. 'That's if you want to talk about it. But, hey, it's not really any of my business.'

'It's okay. I'm getting better at talking about it. It actually helps. There was a time I couldn't tell anyone.'

'Okay,' he said, beginning to eat. 'Spill.'

His easy, matter-of-fact tone relaxed her. She thought back to the drizzly Sunday evening and the interminable drive home. The night that had formed the demarcation line between her past and present life. 'I was on the way back from a weekend training course,' she began slowly. 'I used to be an art teacher, as you may know, and it was a pottery course. The school had recently agreed to fund a kiln, so I went along to learn the basics. It was getting late and was raining. Not much, but enough to make the road slick and slippery.'

Conscious of the conditions and that she was getting tired, she'd slowed down, concentrated more. It was ironic that the accident had happened due to something else entirely.

'I'd just buzzed the window down,' she said, seeing not Eddie and the cosy interior of the pub but instead the gathering twilight of the evening and the rain pattering lightly on her windscreen. 'I was nearly home but getting tired. It was the end of term and a course on top of a tough week's teaching had made me exhausted. The car began to make funny noises.' She attempted a laugh. 'At first I turned the radio up to drown the sound out. I was only ten miles from my flat and prayed I'd get back before breaking down.' She risked a glance at Eddie but his face was carefully expressionless. 'The car was always breaking down.'

'Should have got rid of it.'

'You're not wrong there. Six miles from home the car spluttered to a halt. I was on a dual carriageway, a bit like the one we've just driven on, but it didn't have a hard shoulder. I got it as far off the road as I could, but there was a steep bank upwards on one side, so there was nowhere really to go. I stuck my hazards on, as Dad had drilled into me.'

'Good advice.'

'And then it happened.' Ashley frowned. 'I still can't really understand how. There was hardly anyone else around. Visibility, even though it was getting dark and raining a bit, wasn't bad. I'd reached down to grab my mobile out of my bag to ring the AA and—'

'And?' Eddie prompted gently.

'And a lorry slammed into the back of me.'

'Jeez, Ashley.' He was obviously shocked.

'It's not as bad as it sounds. The lorry driver saw me, but too late. He caught the driver's off-side, shunted me along a little and then skidded to a halt further up the road. The police think he was using his mobile phone. He sent a text about the time of impact. And then when he looked up, it was too late. I was off the carriageway as much as I could be, but he just caught my car. That was enough.'

'Oh my God!'

'I shattered my pelvic girdle and had lacerations to my head.' She put a self-conscious hand to her ear. 'It took a while to get better and I had to learn to walk again.' She shrugged. She was aware Eddie had put down his fork and had stopped eating. He was listening intently. 'So I rely on the stick to keep me balanced.' She flicked her hair over her face. 'And I rely on my hair to hide my scar.'

'You have beautiful hair. *You* are beautiful.'

This time Ashley did blush. 'Th-thank you,' she stammered.

'Thank *you* for telling me. It can't be easy reliving it.' He picked up his fork and pointed it at Ashley's soup. 'Eat before it gets cold.' As they continued with their lunch he added, 'It explains the scar. Do you have flashbacks too? Like that time on the seafront? When the cars ran into each other?'

'Yes.' Ashley blew out a breath. 'Sometimes. It was the noise that time. There's something uniquely horrible and unmistakeable about the sound of a car crash. It took me by surprise too. I can prepare myself for things like today, when I know I have to travel in a car – you know, psyche myself up for it – but that day it was the last thing I was expecting. Too involved in painting, I suppose.' She gave a rueful smile. 'And ignoring you.'

'You have real talent. I couldn't take my eyes off you.' He corrected himself. 'Off your painting, I mean.'

'It was just a study. For something bigger.'

Eddie nodded. 'And you have to make this effort every day? Concentrate on walking. Think through what you might have to face. Prepare yourself?'

'Yes. I suppose I do.'

Eddie leaned back. 'It must be exhausting just living your life.'

Ashley felt relief rush over her. He was the first non-medical person ever to acknowledge this. It was perceptive of him.

'And yet you went ahead and did the interview. That was incredibly brave.'

'Oh come on, I hardly had to go to war, like your

grandfather and Jimmy Larcombe.' Ashley broke off a fragment of the bread bowl. She nibbled it, relieved there were no longer any secrets between them.

'I don't know.' Eddie chuckled. 'Chloe Deverell was a hell of an opponent and, besides, there are all sorts of battles in life. This funeral of Jimmy's – it means a helluva lot to you, doesn't it?'

'Yes, it does.' She put down her spoon, unable to eat any more. 'My great-grandmother died a few years ago, at the grand old age of ninety-seven. She had all of her family around to say goodbye, to celebrate her life. It was only when we were clearing out her room in the nursing home that we found this box. It was full of stuff. Letters from the man she loved and lost in World War Two, a diary where she recounted how she drove buses during the Blitz. She had a whole life before any of us came along that we knew nothing of. Just like your grandfather. I said goodbye to a sweet, stubborn old lady who always slipped me mint imperials. Not the vibrant young woman who lost her sweetheart in a war and drove a bus through the blackout. I suppose what I'm saying is, we write old people off as being just, well, *old*. Not the sum of all they've been throughout their life.'

'Wow,' Eddie said, impressed. 'Quite a speech.'

'And I think that's why sometimes they don't tell us about their lives when they were young. They know we see them as fixed in their role as grandfather or great-aunt or whatever.'

Eddie scraped up the last bit of crab off his plate. 'And, if you're anything like me,' he said ruefully, 'when I was young, I was so self-involved, I couldn't think beyond why my skin erupted right before the crucial date with the hottest girl in eleventh grade.'

Ashley laughed. 'What age would you be in eleventh grade?'

'Sixteen or so.'

'Well, at sixteen, old age is so long away as to be unthinkable. I could never even comprehend being thirty, and yet here I am. You take all that firm body, energy and youth for granted when you're a kid. I know I certainly did before the accident. "Youth is wasted on the young." Isn't that the saying?'

'Yes. It was Oscar Wilde... or was it George Bernard Shaw? Whoever, it's certainly true.' He nodded to her plate. 'You finished? Dessert?'

'I'm not sure I can fit one in,' Ashley said regretfully.

'Not even sticky toffee pudding or spotted dick?' Eddie shook his head. 'That last one kills me. Every time.'

Ashley observed him solemnly. 'Is that the eleventh grader emerging?'

'Yup, probably. I'll go pay, then.'

While he was gone, Ashley stood up and eased her stiff left leg so she was ready to walk again. Their friendship seemed to have shifted up a gear and she liked the fact. She did a few discreet exercises until he was back. Watching him put on his jacket and scarf, she gasped as she remembered. 'This was supposed to be my treat!'

'That decides it. You definitely owe me, Lydden. Another date it is, then. Dinner. You can pay.'

'Okay.' She giggled and accepted his arm as they made their way out of the pub and across the sleet-sparkling road to the car park. 'Once we're back at the flat, please stay for a cup of tea and watch the interview.'

'Nothing would give me greater pleasure.' He went to get in the passenger side, realized, then held the door for her instead, grinning. Going round to the driver's side, he slid in behind the wheel. 'And one other thing.'

'What's that?'

He turned on the ignition and various dials glowed into life. He watched as the sat-nav sprang into action. 'I've renamed Biddy Two. She now goes by the name of Chloe Deverell.'

Ashley giggled on and off all the way home, every time Chloe gave an imperative. It totally took her mind off being a nervous passenger.

# Chapter Fourteen

Noah was at the flat to greet them when they got home. He'd switched on the heating, making the flat cosy and welcoming after their drive through squally, wet snow. 'Ugh, it's vile out there, isn't it? I finished early this arvo, so took the liberty of ordering a takeaway for later. How does Szechuan king prawn, fried soft noodles, crispy duck, prawn toasts and taro croquettes sound? Bottle of fizz in the fridge.' He came to Ashley and ruffled her hair. 'Thought we could celebrate your foray into television!'

'Sounds great to me, but let me get my coat off first.' Ashley shook the wet off and, collecting Eddie's jacket from him, hung them on the hooks in the hall. 'Eddie's staying too. That's okay, isn't it?'

'The more the merrier,' Noah answered cheerfully. 'The Gilded Lion always puts in far too much food.'

'I hope I'm hungry enough for it,' she added, flicking the kettle on. 'We stopped for lunch on the way back.'

'Oh? Where?'

Ashley left them discussing the pub in Sidmouth and went through to her bedroom. It was crowded, as it was where she kept her canvasses when she wasn't working on them. Negotiating several huge ones, thinking she really must get back to painting once the funeral was over, she flopped onto the bed and surveyed her reflection in the mirrored door of the wardrobe. Dark-brown hair, thick and glossy and only frizzing slightly from the damp outside; winter-pale skin marred by a reddened nose from the cold; dark eyes which Piers had always said were her best feature; expressive, mobile eyebrows; a stubborn chin which her mother said came from her father's side of the family and which she shared with Noah. Her cheekbones were too prominent, though, and she was too thin; her collarbone was clearly visible.

She peered closer. But Eddie McQueen had told her she was beautiful. No man had ever said that to her before. Her father called her his beautiful baby girl, but that was different. Piers had admitted she looked hot if she bothered to dress up but had never called her beautiful in the open, matter-of-fact way Eddie had. He'd called her brave too. Wondering if he felt the same about her as she was beginning to feel about him, she basked in the glow of his compliments before hearing Noah call her, saying the tea was poured. She ran a quick brush through her hair, added a spritz of perfume and a slick of lip-gloss and went through to the sitting room, questioning just what she thought she was doing.

Noah had switched on the TV and was sitting on the floor, leaning against the bookshelf. 'We'll catch the end of the national news and then it'll be this *Focus* programme you were on.'

Eddie had resumed his cramped position on the sofa, so Ashley took the mug of tea offered and perched next to him. She couldn't help but be excited. As the national weather forecast finished and the familiar tune for the local magazine programme began, she gripped her mug hard.

Chloe's face appeared on screen, from behind a bright-pink kidney-shaped desk. 'Good evening and welcome,' she said warmly. 'Thank you so much for your company tonight. It's lovely to have you with us.'

Eddie laughed. 'She's a lot friendlier to the camera than she was to you, Ashley.'

'I seem to remember her being quite friendly to you,' Ashley countered with a grin and sipped her tea.

Noah shushed them.

'On tonight's programme,' Chloe continued, 'Exmouth's residents at crisis point with their recycling service, why a war veteran's funeral is going to be the biggest thing to hit Berecombe this year, and a missing parrot is finally reunited with its owner.'

Noah laughed. 'Got to love local news. There you go, Ash, sandwiched between soggy cardboard and Polly the parrot.'

They waited patiently through the report on Exmouth's recyclers being fined for putting the wrong item in the wrong container, and then the camera suddenly switched to the lurid pink sofa that Ashley had had to sit on in the studio. Ashley couldn't stop staring at herself on screen. It was her and yet she looked totally different. She appeared fairly calm and smiley, but the giveaway was the clenched hands in her lap. But she'd been right; she'd been able to get across the important details.

When the interview came to an end, Noah raised his mug in salute. 'Way to go, coz! Brilliant job. You did Jimmy Larcombe and Berecombe proud.' He stood up. 'That should get 'em rolling in. I'll put the plates to warm, shall I? Takeaway should be here any moment.' The doorbell rang. 'Hark! As I speak! I'll go.'

Eddie reached out and took Ashley's hand. 'You did good, kiddo.'

She met his eyes. They were dark and serious in the lamplight. 'Thank you.' And then the moment was shattered by Noah bustling in with several bags of food.

When they'd eaten, and drunk the champagne, Eddie made noises about having to go, but was interrupted by Ashley's phone pinging.

Noah picked it up and threw it to her. 'Text from the studio.'

'Someone's rung in,' Ashley read. 'A Ruby Daniels.' Then she looked up at them, her face shining. 'It says she knew Jimmy Larcombe and wants to come to the funeral!'

'That's great news,' Eddie said. 'You gonna ring her?'

'You should,' Noah added. 'Strike while the iron's hot.'

Ashley looked from one face to the other. 'Well, she's agreed to the studio passing on her number.' She scrutinized it. 'London code, by the look of it.' Before she could talk herself out of it, she began pressing numbers. 'Hello, is that Mrs Ruby Daniels? It's Ashley Lydden here. The *Focus Southwest* studio said it was okay to ring you.'

'Put it on speaker,' Noah whispered.

From the mobile came a wavering voice. 'Hello, my dear. I saw your piece on the news. I always watch *Focus Southwest* even though I'm in London. I get it on my iPad. My Serena set it up for me. When I heard you mention Jimmy Larcombe, I got ever so excited. Then I heard he'd passed away. Poor man. I knew him in the war, you know. I lived with the Larcombes. My, that was a time, I can tell you.'

They could hear a faint voice in the background.

'What's that, Serena? Don't interrupt when I'm on the phone. Oh yes. My daughter's telling me she can bring me down. To Berecombe.' There was a catch in the old woman's voice. 'I'd like to see the place again. I'd like to go to Jimmy's funeral, if you can tell me the details. I'd be ever so grateful.'

Ashley gave them to her, repeating the time and location several times.

'Thank you, dearie. I'm going to try to persuade Serena to take a little holiday. Then we can spend some time in Devon. Haven't been back since the war. Thank you, now. Goodbye.'

Ashley clicked off the phone. 'I can't believe it. Jimmy will have a mourner there, and one who actually knew him too!'

'Well, that's what I call a good end to the evening. Fantastic result, Ash. You going now, Eddie?' Noah added as the man unbent himself from the sofa.

'Guess I'd better.'

'Can I persuade you to help with the putting up of the

patriotic bunting on Saturday?' Noah asked, hopefully. 'We could put you in charge of the Stars and Stripes. Could do with all the help we can get, to be honest. Biddy's bought a shedload of the stuff and her orders are it should all go up. To get the town in the festive spirit.'

'Looks like you've got a volunteer.'

'Wonderful.' Noah looked meaningfully from Ashley to Eddie. 'I'll wash up, shall I? Then you can see our guest to the door. Safe drive home, mate. If it looks icy, feel free to stay over. The sofa-bed is all yours.'

Ashley handed Eddie his jacket and opened the door. A light frost covered everything with a subtle sparkle and a fingernail moon shone clear in an inky night shimmering with stars. It was beautiful. And very cold. She peered into the darkness. 'It's freezing out there. I wish you'd take up Noah's offer of a bed.'

Eddie shrugged on his coat and pulled the collar up against the cold. 'Early start for me tomorrow, so I'd better head home.'

'Drive carefully, won't you?'

He turned to face her. 'Worried about me?' His mouth quirked in humour.

He had a very sensual bottom lip, Ashley decided, getting distracted. God, she was getting in deep here.

'Ashley?' Eddie ducked his head. 'You okay?' His breath misted in the cold air.

Giving herself a shake, she replied, 'I'm fine. Just tired.'

'Well, it's been quite the day. You take care now. Get some rest. Don't let that cousin of yours keep you up with all of his energy.'

'I won't.' When he turned to go, she caught at his sleeve. The leather was warm and buttery-soft to her touch. For a second she wondered what the skin underneath would feel like. 'Please be careful,' she repeated, urgently.

'I promise I'll drive slow and on the right side of the road, ma'am.'

'No!' Then she caught his humour and relaxed. 'Just get yourself back to Berecombe in one piece. We need you.'

He raised one eyebrow. 'And why's that?'

'Well,' she blustered, 'you're tall. You'll come in handy putting the bunting up.'

He leaned in and kissed her cheek softly, his breath warm on her cold skin. 'I'll be here Saturday.'

And then he disappeared into the glistening night, hunching his shoulders against the cold.

## Chapter Fifteen

I n the end, Ashley excused herself from the bunting work party. Balancing on a ladder didn't sound like her idea of fun. Eddie had turned up at the flat early on Saturday morning, with Noah in tow, and she'd made them all bacon and eggs before promising them she'd treat them both to lunch at Millie's later.

Embarrassingly, her appearance on television had turned her into a minor celebrity. As she walked along Berecombe's promenade, people insisted on stopping her, asking wasn't she that girl off the telly and saying what a marvellous thing she was doing. One or two asked if the funeral would be on the *Focus* programme, making her wonder at their motivation for promising to come. It slowed her progress to the café and, by the time she got there, all tables had been taken. Although sunny and bright, it was too breezy to sit outside.

She spotted Biddy and Beryl in pole position in the window, along with a couple of other women she didn't know. Making her way over to them, she asked if she could share their table.

'Of course you can, my lovely,' Beryl said, welcomingly. 'How nice to see you again. And all famous now, after being on the telly! Isn't it a smashing day? A real seasidey day, I always think. With the sun shining and the wind whipping off the sea. The gulls on the wing. Invigorating.'

'Oh, do put a sock in it,' Biddy said. 'Sit down, girl. There's room for a little one.'

Ashley squeezed in between Beryl and an elderly woman she didn't know.

'You might want to say hello to Ruby here,' Biddy said. 'She's been telling us all about how well she knew Berecombe back in the war. Think you need to get her roped into the memories project, young lady.'

Ashley turned to the woman in surprise. 'Ruby? Are you the Mrs Daniels I spoke to on the phone? You're here already. How wonderful. I'm Ashley Lydden.'

The woman was tiny, dressed immaculately in a pale-blue twinset and pearls. Her hair, as white and fluffy as the clouds scudding across the sky over the bay, was coiffed in a shampoo-and-set style. She was everyone's idea of an archetypal granny, until you came to look at the eyes. Bright blue and pin-sharp, they shone with intelligence and a wicked humour.

'Of course you are, dearie,' Ruby said with a chuckle. 'I recognized you as soon as you came in. This is my daughter, Serena.'

A woman in late middle age, and who had the misfortune to be sitting next to Biddy, nodded. Apart from the blue eyes, Ashley couldn't see a resemblance. Serena didn't look happy.

'I can't tell you what a treat it is to be back in Berecombe,' Ruby said. 'It's been ever so many years. Always meant to come back and see the old place but, you know what it's like, life gets busy. Biddy's been explaining all about this museum memory project thing.'

'Ruby has been telling us how the beach was cordoned off with barbed wire,' Biddy boomed.

'Oh yes, I remember that well,' Ruby put in. She giggled. Her voice was much stronger in person than on the phone and she struck Ashley as being an indomitable force, one to be reckoned with. She leaned closer to Ashley. 'One night we'd all had enough of the heat. It was a stuffy May night and none of us could sleep. We sneaked out in our bathers. One of the boys cut a hole in the wire and got through. Had a little paddle and a swim. Heaven, it was.' She laughed again. 'Couldn't see a thing until your eyes got accustomed to the dark. Blackout, you know. Oh, we rejoiced when we could take that down, I can tell you. Like being prisoners in your own home. And the blackout wardens. Some of 'em were right jobsworths. "Put that light out!" they used to yell. There was one we lived in fear of. Mind you, they was only doing their job—'

'I should say so,' Biddy interrupted. 'This part of the coast was ripe for invasion.'

'You're not wrong there, Biddy.' Ruby's face clouded. 'Good times, but we was terrified for most of it.'

Serena patted her mother's hand. 'Don't distress yourself, Mother.' She addressed Ashley. 'I'd like to make it very clear I'm not happy about any of this. Making my mother remember things she should be able to leave in the past. It will be too much for her.' She pursed her lips into a thin, disapproving line. 'She insisted she came to the funeral but I don't want her to have any part in anything else.'

'Don't be daft, child. I'm ninety-one, I'm not in my dotage yet.'

Ashley hid a smile.

Biddy looked around and gestured for Petra to come

over and take their order. 'We'll have another coffee and
then leave you to it, young Ashley. What'll everyone
have? My treat.'

This was so unexpected, Ashley was momentarily lost
for words.

'Come on,' she barked, as Petra approached the table,
pad and pen in hand. 'Hot chocolate?'

'Lovely,' Ashley managed, wondering how it was that
her life had become one surrounded by fierce old ladies
and mainlining hot chocolate in a seaside café. Mind you,
she had no idea how old Biddy actually was. She could
be anything between fifty and ninety.

Petra smiled with an immaculately lipsticked mouth.
She always looked so perfectly groomed, Ashley
thought. Matt foundation, eyeliner in little flicks at the
outer corner of each eye, hair done just so. She didn't
know if the 40s vibe was to match the town's
celebrations or whether it was a lifestyle choice. It
certainly had an effect on the café's sound system;
today Bing Crosby was warbling something about
swinging on a star. Wartime posters had been put up,
one with a buxom blonde who looked not unlike Petra
and which proclaimed, *Keep mum, she's not so dumb!*
Another exhorted: *For a healthy, happy job join the
Women's Land Army.* With yet more patriotic bunting
festooned around, it felt even more 1940s. Ashley half

expected to spot Winston Churchill smoking his cigar in the corner.

'Hello, dearie,' Ruby said. 'What a magnificent victory roll.'

At first Ashley thought Ruby was talking about a type of cake, but when Petra put a hand up to tuck a wisp back into the elaborate roll of blonde hair on top of her head, she sussed what Ruby actually meant. Ashley then noticed the pretty print dress Petra was wearing. It was knee-length with a demure Peter Pan collar and screamed 1940s. Definitely a lifestyle choice, then. No one would go to that much bother otherwise. As Petra was tiny but curved in and out in all the right places, it suited her.

'Thank you,' she said, smiling even more broadly. 'Not many people recognize it.'

Ruby winked. 'It was all the rage when I was a girl. I used to try to get mine like it, but my hair was too fine. Used to just flop right back down again. I'd like a pot of tea, please,' she added decisively. 'And a teacake, with lots of butter. And the same for my daughter.'

As they waited for their order, Ashley filled them all in on the television interview and the astonishing response. 'I've had about a thousand messages in two days,' she said. 'I think it's safe to say Jimmy will have a funeral the town can be proud of.'

'Sounds like you're doing a grand job, young Ashley,' Biddy said.

Beryl stared in astonishment. Ashley guessed a compliment from Biddy was a rarity. 'Thank you, Biddy. That means a lot.'

Then talk turned to news of the latest cut in bus services, and Biddy and Beryl grumbled about how difficult it made it to get around without a car. Ashley found herself agreeing with them. Being reliant on public transport had made her aware of its limitations. With a wry smile, she realized she was identifying with the concerns of two elderly women.

Petra returned and served them with a neat precision. 'Enjoy, ladies!'

As she walked away, Ashley noticed the seamed stockings and glossy high heels. 'How does she work all day wearing those shoes?' she marvelled.

'Smashing pair of pins,' Ruby said, admiringly. 'We didn't have stockings in the war. Well, not until the Yanks came. When I went out I painted lines on my legs in gravy browning. Used to run when it rained!'

'Did you wear your hair in a victory roll, Beryl?' Biddy asked with apparent innocence, stirring her coffee and probably a lot more besides.

'Have a heart, Bid. As you well know, I was a baby in

the war. Would have looked a bit daft with nappies and a knitted buster suit.'

Biddy sniffed. 'Time was, you were known for wearing a lot less. I remember talk of you posing nude on top of a tractor in Berecombe Harbour. What were you called for a bit? "No Knickers Noreen", wasn't it?'

'I'd watch my mouth if I was you, Biddy Roulestone,' Beryl replied tartly. 'If we're taking that road of conversation, I remember who it was who fed the WI marijuana-laced chocolate brownies.'

Biddy lifted her coffee cup with an air of insouciance. 'And I seem to remember them going down very well.'

'Until they found out what was in them,' Beryl cackled and winked at Ashley.

Ruby joined in. 'Supposed to be good for arthritis, isn't it? Amongst other things.' She shifted on the hard wooden chair. 'You might have to get me the recipe, Biddy.'

'Mother!' Serena said, shocked.

Ruby turned to her daughter. 'What's the matter, Serena?' Pursing her thin lips at Biddy and Beryl, she added, 'Always the same with the young 'uns, isn't it? They think they invented sex, drugs and rock and roll.'

As the table erupted into laughter, Ashley fought to keep a straight face. Noah would do better to forget the memories project and record this double act instead. And it looked as if they'd found a perfect third wheel with Ruby. She buried her giggles in her hot chocolate.

'Hey guys, what's all this hilarity?' It was Eddie.

'What's the matter, Mother?' Serena asked, as Ruby's laughter stopped abruptly. 'You've gone as white as a sheet.'

# Chapter Sixteen

Ashley looked up in alarm. Ruby's eyes were fixed on Eddie. Gone was the mischievous pensioner. In her place was a vulnerable woman looking the entirety of her years, if not more.

Eddie squeezed in next to Ashley, saying, 'Noah's gone to the counter to order.' Laughing, he added, 'Think it's an excuse to chat to Petra.'

Serena patted her mother's arm. 'Mum, are you all right?'

Ruby went to lift her teacup but it rattled on its saucer so much, she changed her mind. 'Sorry, lovie. Someone walked on my grave. I'm fine. Don't fuss.'

Ashley introduced Eddie and, as Noah had managed to tear himself away from Petra and come to stand by their table, explained who he was too. She was glad to see Ruby's colour returning.

'An American, then?' Ruby asked beadily. She managed to drink some tea but her eyes didn't leave Eddie.

'Yes, ma'am.'

'And what are you doing over here, then?'

'Mother! Don't be so rude.'

Eddie gave Serena a charming smile which deepened his dimple. 'No problem. Reasonable enough question. I teach at the university. History.'

Biddy stood up suddenly. 'And we'll be history too if we don't go. I said I'd help sort the jumble in the Masonic Hall and there's a mountain of the stuff. You coming, Beryl?'

'Better had.' She drained her coffee and shrugged on her bright-pink jacket. 'Nice seeing you again, Ashley, and you too, Eddie and Noah. And hope to see you around the town, Ruby and Serena.'

'We'll be at the funeral,' Serena added, starchily. 'Of course.'

'Of course,' Beryl said cheerfully. 'We'll see you there, then. Bye all.' She trotted after Biddy who was already marching along the promenade.

Noah took her chair. 'I've taken the liberty of ordering us lunch, Ash. That okay?'

'Fine. And it's my treat, remember?'

'No argument here.'

'Has all the bunting gone up?'

Noah grinned. 'The entire town is plastered. Everything that didn't move got decorated. Actually, one or two things that did move got covered too. Two strands of everything. Union Flag and Stars and Stripes. That's to welcome our American guests,' he explained to Ruby.

Ashley saw her stiffen. There was definitely something about all things American that bothered the old lady. She spooned up a marshmallow and watched the emotions flit across Ruby's face. Whatever it was, her daughter didn't share it or know anything about it; Serena was sitting slightly apart from them, superiority coming off her in waves.

'I understand you're here to attend Jimmy Larcombe's funeral,' Noah said to Ruby. 'Being in the town must bring back a lot of memories.'

Ashley winced. It wasn't the most subtle of comments. She thought he could have eased off the project for at least one day.

Ruby drank some tea and took her time to answer. 'I haven't been back since the war.'

'Oh my goodness. Has the place changed much? I've only been living here since last autumn and Ashley here only arrived a few weeks ago. We're newcomers.' Noah gave Ruby the benefit of his most charming smile.

'Blow-ins, they call you,' Ruby huffed. 'Called me a lot worse when I arrived, I can tell you.'

Noah accepted the coffee Petra served him. 'And when was that?' He stirred it casually but Ashley knew her cousin well enough to tell he was on high alert.

'Got here in 1939. September it was, when I piled off the train.'

'You were an evacuee?'

'You don't have to answer any of these questions, Mother.' Serena put a protective hand on Ruby's arm.

'Oh, save your breath to cool your porridge, Serena. I don't mind.' She fixed Noah with a penetrating look from her birdlike eyes. 'Makes a change to have folk interested. Some forget we've had a whole life and lived most of it well before you lot was born.'

'I can assure you, I'm not at all like that,' Noah protested. 'You see, I'm heading up a memories project and I'd very much like to interview you as part of it. Your wartime experiences in Berecombe would be an invaluable addition.'

Ruby's lips twitched with humour. Ashley was certain the old woman was playing Noah.

'I know about your project. Biddy and Beryl told me all about it. And I know why you're asking your questions,' Ruby added, with a twinkle that was positively flirtatious. 'It isn't because you're interested in *me*. I expect what you're really after is some juicy titbit for your museum.'

*Round one to Ruby,* Ashley thought. She was making Noah work hard for what he wanted. She caught Eddie's eye and giggled at his mouthed 'Ouch.'

To be fair to Noah, he didn't seem put out. Leaning back, he gave a shamefaced grin. 'Touché. I apologize for underestimating you and not being more transparent. But you're wrong on one point. I am interested in you as a person, as well as capturing your memories for the project. Something tells me you have quite a story to tell.'

'Well, young Noah, I just might.'

'So, Mrs Daniels, I'm asking you, formally and with the greatest of respect, whether you would take part in the project while you're here. It would mean a great deal to me.'

Ashley could see Ruby softening. Most women did in the face of Noah's charm offensive.

'I'll do it,' the old woman said. 'But only if Ashley and this American bloke here is with me.'

'I'd love to tag along,' Eddie said. 'It would be a genuine pleasure to hear your memories, ma'am.'

A wistful look overcame Ruby's thin face. 'Ma'am.

That takes me back. That's what they used to call Jimmy's mum.'

Ashley squeezed Ruby's hand. 'And, as I'm the one who is responsible for you being here, you can count on me. And I promise you, and your daughter too,' she added, as she saw Serena's anxious expression, 'that if anything upsets you we'll stop straight away.'

'Right then,' Ruby said. 'When do you want to start?'

To everyone's astonishment, Noah brought out his handheld recorder. 'Never go anywhere without it,' he said as he grinned.

## Chapter Seventeen

'Mam was worried silly about all the bombs,' Ruby began. 'Or the threat of them. That and the gas. Everyone thought the Germans would gas us like they did in the last show, you see. She suffered with her nerves, as we used to say back then. We sat round the radio, me and her, and listened to Chamberlain tell us we was at war, like the rest of the country. And, like the rest of the country, we fretted about what was going to happen. Mam burst into tears, and I got into trouble for finding the embroidered hankie to give to her to mop her up. She was saving it for best, she said. I was twelve then.' She frowned. 'Yes, not far off thirteen. Never seen my Mam cry before. Didn't know what to do. She saw the funny side in the end. Said what was the point of keeping things for best if ruddy Hitler was going to gas us all?

'Kiddies began to leave straight away. A lot had gone even before war was declared. It all happened very quick. Mam had been at Paddington with Mrs Wicke from next door. She'd seen what happened when they all went. Whole classes at a time from my school, with their teacher, off onto a train to goodness knows where, with just a suitcase and a bar of chocolate. No one knew, you see, where they'd end up. Mrs Wicke's little Stan was only six and a real baby. Broke her heart to see him go. Didn't stop crying for a week. And it was all of a month later before she found out he was with a family on a farm near Taunton. Mam said she didn't want that for me. So yes, you were right.' Ruby addressed Noah. 'I was an evacuee but not one who went with the rest of the school.' She smiled sadly. 'There's a part of me that thinks I might have liked that. At least you was with your school pals and your teachers. You knew a few folk. The way it happened with me, I didn't know a soul.'

'What happened, Ruby?' Ashley asked gently. 'How did you end up in Berecombe?'

'Mam had a distant cousin. Florrie. Married a Berecombe man. She wrote and asked if they'd take me in. So I got the train, all on my own, told not to speak to no one, counted the fields to pass the time. Never seen anything so green. So green, it sounded loud. And the air! It was that fresh when I got off the train at Axminster that it fair knocked me off my feet. And that's when I met Jimmy. He'd cadged a lift with the doctor's car to come and pick me up. My Auntie Florrie married John Larcombe, you see, and Jimmy was their son. Just going on twenty. Thin streak of bacon, he was. All gangly long legs and arms. The doctor and Jimmy collected me all up and brought me here, to Berecombe. First time I'd seen the sea. Even with all the barbed wire and the concrete tank traps on the beach and the gun emplacement up there on the cliff, I fell in love. It was the light. Shimmering off the water and hitting your eyes so hard, it made them tear up. And the smell. All fishy and salty but something else too. Fresh and light and full of goodness. You just wanted to gasp it all in. The poor old Thames only ever smelled of mud.'

Ruby drank the rest of her tea, which must by now have been stone cold. She dabbed at the corner of her mouth delicately. 'And here I stayed until—' She paused. 'Until I was old enough for war work, and then I went back to London.' She laughed. 'I'd missed all the fun they had, all right. Mam said the doodlebugs were the things that scared her most.' She fixed her eyes on Ashley. 'It was when the noise stopped, you see. That's when it had run out of fuel and you knew it was coming for you.

Mam said Hitler never gassed us all because he had far worse planned. After a wobbly start, I'd settled into life in Berecombe, then went back to London rolling my "r"s like a good old Devon girl. Didn't fit in there neither. Hadn't been through what they'd been through, had I? Besides, Mam had seen a little girl of twelve off. She met a young woman off the train at Paddington. I'd done all my growing up here. Don't think she knew what to do with me.'

'Didn't your mother ever visit?' Ashley asked.

Ruby shook her head. 'Too busy, I think. She'd got night work at the munitions factory. The trains could be difficult. You never knew which line had been bombed. Journeys took bloomin' ages. By the time she got here, it would be time to go back.' Ruby wrinkled her nose. 'Got a feeling she was enjoying her freedom too. No kid around, no husband. Despite everything, she was having a good time.'

'What about your father? You haven't mentioned him,' Noah asked.

Ruby turned to Noah in surprise, as if she'd forgotten he was there. 'My dad? I didn't have one. He ran off when I was a baby. Couldn't cope with Mam's heebie-jeebies. So Mam parked me where she thought I'd be safe and with someone she sort of knew, and got on with her life.' She sat back. 'So that's how I ended up here.' She glanced at Serena, who was ashen. 'Don't take on so. It was what we did. It was what we all had to do. And it wasn't so horrible once the bullying stopped.'

'Bullying?' Serena said faintly.

'The local kids. Didn't like having their school disrupted, I suppose. Too many of us all to fit into the schoolroom, so we was schooled in shifts. Locals in the morning, evacuees in the afternoon. That's when I went, in the afternoon. Or I did til I was old enough to serve in Auntie Florrie's shop. Ooh, I loved working in that shop. Got to know everyone.'

'What did it sell?' Noah asked.

'It was a grocer's, so a bit of everything. As long as you had the rations for it, of course.' Ruby smiled dreamily. 'Used to love weighing out the sugar into tiny little twists of paper. Jimmy helped too, but most of the time he was out on his uncle's boat. Jimmy loved the sea. He would have made fishing his livelihood, I think, if things had been different. As it was, all the bigger boats were requisitioned, and Jimmy and his Uncle Reg had to dodge all sorts when they were out. Mines and the like. They had to keep inshore. Once they scooped up a pilot. He'd bailed. They picked him out of the water, Mae West an' all. Brought him back into the harbour and the harbour master and policeman took him off to hospital. Reg boasted it was his best catch.

Not that we saw much of the fish he and Jimmy caught.'

'Was fish rationed?' Ashley said.

'No, dearie. But it was very expensive. We didn't eat much of it. Not even fish and chips. Couldn't get the fat to fry it, you see. It was a treat when we did have it, though. All hot and vinegary.' Ruby turned to her daughter. 'And I could eat some right now!'

'We'll get some before we go back to the bed and breakfast, then.' Serena smiled. 'We'll share a portion, as you know it gives you heartburn.'

Ruby heaved herself to her feet, waiting until the stiffness had gone from her legs. Obviously she'd had enough of the memories session. She pouted like a little girl. 'I tell you,' she said to her audience, 'growing old isn't for sissies. I'm as stiff as a board. Come on, Serena, grab me arm and lead me to those chips. I know they probably do them in here, but I want proper fish and chips – hot as hell, nice and salty, with a big battered cod!'

## Chapter Eighteen

After the two women had left, Petra came over and asked if they were ready for lunch. 'I didn't like to interrupt before. All looked very intense.'

Noah blew out a breath. 'Oh lordy, you can say that again.' He rubbed his hands together. 'We've got ourselves some dynamite. Solid dynamite!'

'Certainly knocks tales from the allotments into perspective,' Ashley agreed. 'Think we're going to have something really worth preserving from Ruby. And she's a natural storyteller. I felt I was almost with her when she glimpsed her first view of the sea and the beach. Although I have no idea what a tank trap is.'

'It's what it says on the tin. Usually a line of concrete blocks built into the sand to stop enemy tanks in the instance of invasion. It was a very real threat along this coast, especially in the early years of the war.'

Ashley shuddered. 'I can't imagine living with that fear. This would have been the front line, had they succeeded.'

'Oh yes, the Stop Line is just a little inland from here. It was to defend the rest of the country if the Germans landed. The idea being, they'd get so far inland and no further. But if you were right on the coast, as we are here, well...' Noah let the sentence hang.

'Doesn't bear thinking about,' Petra said. 'I'll go and get your lunch and you can concentrate on food instead. Fries, tuna melts and roasted red-pepper soup coming right up.'

'So,' Eddie said, as he bit into his panini five minutes later. 'What else can we expect from Ruby? Do you think there was anything between her and Jimmy?'

'Didn't Ruby say she was only twelve? Jimmy was much older.' Noah grabbed a chip and dunked it in his soup. 'She must have been lonely here. At least if you were evacuated with your classmates, you had your friends around.'

'I expect Ruby had a crush on Jimmy,' Ashley said, thoughtfully. 'You know, hero worship. Looking up to the older figure.'

'Speaking from experience, coz? Did you hero worship me?'

Ashley looked at Noah. 'How could I resist you?' she deadpanned. 'And it's never gone away. I mean, look at you now, with soup dribbled all down your shirt.'

'Is it? Oh hell.' Noah scrubbed ineffectually at the stain with a paper serviette. 'And I've got a cinema meeting at four.' He leaped up and made for the toilet. 'I'll go and try to wash it off. You two carry on. Won't be a tick.'

'No chance of stopping me eating,' Eddie said. 'I'm starving. All that going up and down ladders. My body's a wreck.'

Ashley sincerely doubted it. She crunched on a chip. 'Where has the bunting gone up?'

'Where hasn't it! All along main street.'

'The high street?'

Eddie grinned. 'There too. All along the promenade. Around the square in front of the theatre and across the front of the museum, naturally.'

'Naturally.'

'Around the front of the café and bookshop here, and we had some left over, so Noah suggested we string it along the fencing by the river. I had no idea that river walk was there. It's awesome.'

'It is. I've been meaning to go there and paint

141

sometime.' Ashley nibbled her tuna melt. 'Amazingly, I haven't had the time. My days get filled up quite quickly lately.' It wasn't completely true; she found herself exhausted after the easiest of tasks and had to remember to pace herself, as she was still convalescing. She kept having to remind Noah too. He had now got her sifting through some ancient paper files in the museum. She tired after even an hour.

'Maybe it'll go quieter once the funeral's over?'

'Hopefully. Will you come?'

'If I can. I'm getting behind with some uni work, so I'll have to see.'

'Chloe said something about the possibility of a TV crew covering it for the *Focus* programme.' She winced.

'You don't approve? Or is it the thought of rubbing up against the affable Ms Deverell again?'

'I don't want Jimmy's funeral to become a circus, that's all.'

'How many can the church hold?'

Ashley blinked. 'I couldn't tell you. Two hundred, maybe? It's the little town church, the one with the Norman tower tucked up behind the street the museum is on, in the old part of town.'

'Maybe have a chat with the vicar about speakers. If the congregation spills out into the churchyard, they can listen from there.'

'Good idea.' Ashley frowned. 'But I really hope it doesn't come to that.' She swallowed. 'Oh Eddie, what have I done?'

Eddie took her hand and held it for a warming second. 'You've done a man proud, is all.' He resumed eating, asking, 'Where's the wake?'

'Here. The WI have swung into action.'

'That means Biddy?'

'Yes, okay, Biddy has swung into action. Several urns of tea, copious amounts of sandwiches and cakes. I just hope she doesn't supply her famous brownies.'

'Why's that?'

'She puts hash in them.'

Eddie laughed so much that he began to choke and Ashley had to whack him on the back quite hard. 'Whatta gal,' he exclaimed, once he got his breath back.

Noah returned just then, the soup stain reduced to a damp patch, and chimed in, misunderstanding their conversation, 'That's my Ash. She's one hell of a girl.' Sitting down, he added, 'That reminds me. I have something to ask.' He picked up his sandwich and bit into it innocently.

Ashley gave Eddie an eloquent look. 'I always know a compliment from my cousin means one thing and one thing only.'

'What's that?' Eddie asked with a grin.

'That he's after a favour. Another one!'

'Well, it's not so much a favour, seeing as Ruby specifically asked for you two to be present when she's recording her memories,' Noah protested. 'I mean, I'm going to be terribly tied up with meetings and other things. The tea party to welcome the GIs, for instance...' he tailed off.

'So you'd like us to tape Ruby's sessions,' Ashley finished.

'Oh, would you? I rather think you'd get more out of her than me.'

'Of course I will, but Eddie here has a proper job. He may not be able to find the time.'

'Oh, don't worry about me. I'll check back with the university and may even be able to log it in with my usual stuff. I'd be happy to help you out, Ashley.' He gave her a look that sent heat straight to her face. 'And you, Noah, of course. Although, Ruby went kinda strange on me when she found out I was from the States.'

'She did, didn't she?' Ashley said. 'I'd love to get to the bottom of that.'

'Maybe it's something to do with the GIs?' Noah suggested. 'They pretty much flooded the area. They estimate there were about eighty thousand across Dorset and east Devon. It would have made a huge impact on the local population.'

'Especially to a young girl like Ruby,' Ashley added. 'When did they arrive?'

'1943. November, according to what I've found out about my grandfather,' Eddie put in. 'I suppose Ruby would have been about fifteen or sixteen.'

'A young girl and all these glamorous Yanks around. Bound to make an impression.' Noah pulled a face. 'They used to say of them, "Overpaid, oversexed and over here."'

'Now that's what I call a recipe for hero worship,' Ashley said and they laughed.

## Chapter Nineteen

The day of Jimmy's funeral dawned bright and cool, with a glassy blue sky and scudding white clouds.

Noah dropped Ashley off at the church saying, 'Sorry it's so early but I really need to check in at the museum first.' He gave her a quick peck on the cheek. 'Will see you later and don't look so worried. It's all going to be fine.'

As Ashley stood in front of the deserted church, she wished she shared Noah's optimism. Self-consciously, she tugged at the navy wool dress that had been the only suitable funeral wear in her wardrobe. She didn't wear dresses very often and her legs, in their matte tights, felt horribly exposed. Pulling the grey wrap more closely around her, she considered what to do. She was very early and there was no one in sight. 'Well, Jimmy,' she said to the chilly air as a blackbird took fright and startled her. 'No madding crowds just yet, but let's just hope a few people will turn up later.'

Deciding moving was the only option to keep warm, she wandered around the side of the church, heading for a patch of early morning sun. She wasn't looking forward to the actual funeral for a number of reasons and not just her concerns over whether anyone would turn up. To her delight, she soon found herself on rising ground and with a magnificent view of the eastern end of the bay. Even better, there was a bench in a patch of thin sunlight but sheltered from the breeze by an elderly yew. Her fingers itched for her paints and she promised herself that she would return and capture the scene in front of her another day. Wrapping her frozen fingers in her shawl, she lifted her face to the sun, enjoying the birdsong and the faint rustle of some unseen and unknown creature going about its business. The blackbird hopped out of a bush, eyed her, decided she posed no threat and carried on hunting. Ashley closed her eyes and drank in the peace.

It had been a hectic few days. Ashley had liaised with Erica and Andrea about the programme of service, the music, the possibility of setting up a sound system. Then there'd been a flurry of calls with Petra and Biddy about the catering and, unexpectedly, she'd had to arrange, of all things, some Morris dancers for the wake. Andrea had just remembered Jimmy had been a great friend of the local 'side' and thought it would add a nice touch. It intrigued Ashley how pieces of Jimmy's life were jig-sawing together from all the people he'd known in different phases of his life. The TV appearance had continued to encourage queries about the funeral. Some were obviously not genuine but one email had got her very excited. It was from a cousin of Jimmy's, the daughter of his Uncle Reg who she now knew he had liked to fish with. Peggy Crawford was coming all the way from Northumberland and was bringing her entire family. 'So Jimmy,' Ashley murmured as her friend the blackbird cackled. 'As well as your old friend Ruby, you'll have real family here.'

'Talking to yourself, now? Has the strain finally got to you?'

Her eyes flew open to see Eddie standing tall in front of her.

'I'd say it was morbid sitting in a churchyard, but one with a view like this, I guess I'll have to let you off.' He sat down beside her and she felt the heat coming from his body. It was all she could do not to cuddle into him. 'This town, eh?' He shook his head. 'Full of surprises. One round every corner. I had no idea this was here.'

'Nor me. It's wonderful, isn't it? You missed the best bit. I caught the tail end of the most marvellous sunrise. The sky and water all turned into this shimmery oyster-greyish-pink. It was extraordinary. What?' She turned to him. 'Are you laughing at me?'

He met her gaze and stared penetratingly. 'I'd never laugh at you, Ashley. You must know that.' Then he smiled. 'I'm simply wondering how you saw all that with your eyes closed.'

'I just rested them for a moment. It's been quite the week.' And then she quite forgot what to say next. He had green lights in his hazel eyes, luxuriant dark lashes and deep creases of humour at the outer corners. The intelligent face of someone who saw the humour in as many aspects of life as possible.

He took her hand. 'I bet. I'm sorry I couldn't help more. You okay, Ashley?'

She forced herself to breathe normally. 'Yes, I'm fine. What have you been doing? Catching up with university work?'

Eddie nodded then frowned. 'Jeez, your hand is frozen.' He reached for the other one and held them within his own, chafing them. 'What are you doing sitting out in the cold like this?'

'Oh, I'm tough. British, you know. Used to a bit of cold. Not like you Americans.'

He laughed. 'Someday I'll put you right about an east coast winter. Now, however, is not the time. I came looking for you. Your vicar, Erica, has just gone in to put the heating on and there are already quite a few people turning up. She said she'd save us a seat near the front.'

'Oh, do we have to go?' She spoke without thinking. She could sit and talk to him forever. How had this happened? She was in way too deep before even realizing she'd got there. A beat of longing held in the air.

'I suppose we better had.' He gave her a long look. 'It's Jimmy's funeral. The one you've been working so hard on.'

Ashley shook her head. 'Sorry, of course. I only meant it's such a shame to move from this view,' she added, lamely.

'The view won't go anywhere. We can come back another time, if you'd like?' He stood up and held a hand out to her. 'Maybe for another sunrise?'

She took it. 'I'd like that very much.' Standing, she felt breathless and giddy at his nearness. He was wearing a formal suit, the crisp white shirt and the deep grey of the jacket contrasting with his smoothly tanned skin. He looked better than any sea view and she knew which she'd rather stare at.

'You sure you're okay? You said yourself you've had a tough week.' He tucked her hand under his arm and they began walking towards the main entrance of the church. 'No stick?'

'No, I thought I'd try without it today.' To undermine her words, she promptly tripped on a loose stone.

'Hey, steady there. I think you've been overdoing it.'

Eddie's arm came around her back, holding her close. Ashley leaned into him, half resenting how much she needed to, half swooning at how good he smelled.

He turned her to him and ran a thumb down her cheek, his eyes dark. Time fractured and the universe waited for them to make the decision.

Cupping her neck, he pulled her closer. 'I have no right to do this,' he murmured, his mouth hesitating over hers. 'I shouldn't do this. But jeez, Ashley, you've got a way of getting under a man's skin. You're driving me wild.'

She lifted her mouth to his and sweetness and desire took over. His arm tightened around her and she arched her back to press her breasts against him. Sliding her hands under his suit jacket, she found heat and muscle and let an animal cry escape. Opening to him, the kiss deepened, threatening to get out of control.

It seemed to go on for ever and be over in a second. Breaking apart, they stared at each other, wide-eyed. Ashley, her lips on fire, put a hand to his chest. Eddie's heart was racing and his tanned skin flushed; he looked as shocked as she felt.

'This makes no sense. We hardly know each other,' she whispered. 'It's mad.'

'I know I want you,' he answered, his voice ragged.

'And I want you,' Ashley said quickly, heat and lust pounding through her. She reached up to claim his mouth again. He tasted of mint and desire, and she wanted more. She tucked her cold fingers under Eddie's shirt in a desperate search to inch closer into him.

'I've got to stop this,' he said against her mouth, his voice hoarse, his breath ragged.

Ashley shifted away reluctantly. 'Definitely not the right time or place,' she agreed, trying to use humour to deflate the situation.

He lifted ironic eyebrows. 'You could say that. But there's something I need to talk over with you as well.' Running a hand around the back of his collar, he gave her a rueful look and then glanced at his watch. 'We'd better go.'

'Better had.'

She waited until he'd straightened his tie and collar and then began to walk away.

He caught her hand. 'Unfinished business?'

She registered the blaze in his eyes and nodded. 'Unfinished business.'

As they neared the corner of the church, she could hear the low murmur of voices, with the odd punctuation of a louder one as someone recognized a long-lost friend.

'Are you prepared, Ashley?' Eddie asked. 'You wanted Jimmy to have a few mourners to bid him his last goodbye.' They rounded the corner and he gave her a quick hug, 'I think you might have succeeded.'

The wide square space in front of the church was full. People of all ages and sexes filled it. Most were sombrely dressed, a few in uniform. Ashley recognized the RNLI crew, the Tizzard family out in force, several suited men who could only be from the council, Biddy and her WI members, Petra chic in black and white spots, Andrea and the care home staff, and Ruby and Serena right at the front. Filling the twisting path down to the lane were many more people. There must have been at least two hundred people there, if not more.

'They've all come,' she whispered, ridiculous tears starting. She turned to him. 'Oh Eddie, everybody's come!'

'Of course they have! You done good, kiddo.' Then he took her by the shoulders and kissed her again.

For a second, despite everything, despite being at a funeral and in full sight of a large crowd, she responded.

'Ash, I've got to talk to you about this—' he began but got no further.

'Ashley!' Erica yelled. She ran over, her clerical robes flying behind. Taking Ashley's hands in hers, she added, 'What a turn-out! Oh Ashley, Jimmy would have loved this!'

## Chapter Twenty

Ashley and Eddie squeezed in on the far side of the second pew. He kept her hand in his. The skin contact was electric and she wanted to hold his hand forever. An unspoken heat throbbed between them. Ashley dared to look into his eyes and was warmed further by the emotion she saw there. She shivered slightly and he tucked her hand into his suit pocket. It lay there like a promise.

Despite Erica claiming she had put on the heating, the old squat church was freezing, with a cold so palpable, it felt as solid as the thick stone walls. Ashley felt her nose turn to ice so was doubly glad of Eddie's large, warm presence next to her, even though it made concentration difficult.

The service was sweet. Poignant but with a sense of

celebration for a man who had lived long and well. Erica began with the eulogy. 'A local man through and through,' she said. 'Never far from the sea. Having returned from World War Two, he continued to serve his town with a job at the council and for the RNLI. He retired to a bungalow and an impeccably tended garden, was a keen fundraiser for several local charities and an active member of the local folk scene. Jimmy was a good neighbour. A kind man.'

It was a very ordinary life, Ashley thought, and yet, looking around at all those who had crammed themselves into the church, Jimmy Larcombe had reached out to many.

Andrea spoke next, saying that Jimmy had been a mischievous member of the care home, always ready with a joke, and had joined in with whatever was organized. 'He had a go at anything,' she said. 'Pottery, crochet, and he was particularly fond of our resident cat who always made a beeline for his lap, knowing she'd have a warm welcome and endless cuddles.' Andrea stopped and Ashley was touched to see her dab at her eyes. 'I'm not supposed to have favourites,' she added, with a sniffle, 'but Jimmy was one. He made coming in for a shift at work something to look forward to, and I will really miss him. To use his own words, "You're going to miss me when I've gone." It's very true. Rest in peace, gentle man.'

She returned to her seat and Erica asked if anyone else wanted to say a few words. An elderly woman was helped up. 'I'm Peggy,' she said, in a frail voice that could barely be heard. 'I'm the daughter of Jimmy's Uncle Reg, so I'm Jimmy's first cousin. Dad never felt the same about the sea after Dunkirk, so he moved away from Berecombe to Hexham. I was a late baby and we never came south to visit, so I never knew Jimmy in person. At my age, though, you start to really value and appreciate the family you have left in a new way, so when my grandson saw the article on Facebook and told me about it, I knew I had to be here today.' She smiled, illuminating her creased face. 'Ee, it's that grand to be able to say goodbye to him. I know Dad would be made up to see so many at his nephew's funeral; they were very close at one point. Rest in peace, our Jimmy.'

Ashley was intrigued. Something Biddy had said came back to her – that Jimmy had been at Dunkirk. They stood to sing 'The Lord's My Shepherd' and Ashley caught sight of an emotional Ruby being helped to her feet by Serena. She only had the haziest of knowledge about what happened at Dunkirk and resolved to ask Ruby if she knew anything about Jimmy's involvement.

At the end of the service Ruby came to the front of the

church and Ashley watched as she laid a trembling hand on the coffin. The old woman whispered something and then mopped her face with her handkerchief, so overcome that Serena had to help her back to a pew.

They emerged from the church into blissfully warm spring sunshine. Ashley spotted Chloe from *Focus Southwest* thrusting her woolly microphone at a good-looking member of the RNLI crew and a cameraman nosing in for a shot. They had turned up after all. She slipped her hand through Eddie's arm. 'Have you brought your car?' she asked urgently.

'Yes. Trains weren't the right timings to get here for the funeral. Why?'

'Would you mind giving me a lift to Millie's?'

'Don't you want to stay for the interment?'

'I could do with getting to the café to check everything's set up.' She glanced at the ominous hole dug in the graveyard, all ready for the coffin. 'Besides, I loathe when they throw earth onto the coffin.' She shuddered. 'Jimmy won't lack for mourners,' she added, watching as the crowd began to make its way to the graveside.

'Sure. Okay. I'm parked just over there.'

They drove the short distance in silence. It was almost as if the kiss had never happened. With a suppressed sigh, Ashley put it down to all the heightened emotion that had been around. Unwilling to bring the subject up, she let him concentrate on squeezing into a tight parking space on the road that ran parallel to the promenade.

Eddie pulled on the handbrake, switched off the ignition and turned to her. The morning sun lightened his hair and bathed him in warmth, but his eyes were guarded. 'You okay? What was the real reason for leaving?'

She forced a brief smile. 'Oh, I don't know. Intimations of my own mortality. Not wanting to encounter Chloe Deverell again. Really not wanting to see a coffin being lowered into the ground.' So he wasn't going to mention what had happened between them either. She straightened her shoulders. 'The doctors once let it slip that I came close to death in the accident. I'm not too good at funerals. At the actual burial. Brings it back, I suppose.'

'Understandable.' He put a reassuring hand on her arm, making her skin hum. 'You did good back there.'

'Thank you.'

'And now what you need is a cup of tea.'

Ashley forced out a giggle. 'Think you're becoming a true Brit.'

He reached over to her and for one intoxicating moment the possibility of another kiss hung in the air. He went to say something, then changed his mind and just grinned and waggled his eyebrows. 'I'm kind of getting a liking for the British way of doing things. I'm kind of getting fond of most things over here.'

Ashley pulled a face as a response. 'Don't know how to break it to you, but I don't think the next few hours are going to give you any kind of indication about how we do an English funeral. What with Biddy's catering and Morris dancers providing the entertainment, it's going to be completely surreal.'

'All the better. We need more eccentricity in this world.'

She couldn't leave what had happened between them before the funeral. It was itching at her like a half-healed scab. 'You said you needed to talk to me about something?' she asked hopefully.

Eddie blew out a breath and stared hard at the sun bouncing off the promenade. 'Not sure we've got enough time right now. It's complicated. It's about a woman I worked with. We taught alongside one another and I was in love with her for years.'

Ashley's heart sank. This wasn't what she'd hoped to hear. 'Did she know?'

'Oh yes, Bree knew,' Eddie said, frowning. 'I came out

here to try to forget all about her, but it's not that simple; she's looking after my dog. He was too sick to come with me, so she volunteered. She keeps texting me, asking about medication, whether she needs to take him to the vet. I guess I'll have to see her when I go back home. I'm desperate to see poor old Bowie.'

Ashley wasn't sure what he was telling her. 'Well of course you'd want to see your dog,' she said briskly and unclipped her seatbelt. Her hand rested on the door handle. She needed to know what he'd meant, if anything, by the kiss. She'd felt the passion burning from him; there was no mistaking that. 'But, you don't have any feelings for Bree now, is that what you're saying?'

Eddie shook his head. 'No, I don't have feelings for her, not anymore, but she's toxic, Ash. She's trouble. And there's something else going on with her that she's not saying. I know her well enough to sense that.' He reached for her arm. 'I want to sort it out, I *need* to sort it out before this – us – goes any further.'

She stared at him. 'Of course,' she said crisply. 'I understand.' But she didn't. She didn't understand at all and, at the moment, she had other things she had to do. Swallowing her fear that the little bit of happiness they'd built between them was about to be snatched away, she added, 'We'd better get going, hadn't we?'

## Chapter Twenty-One

As it turned out, Ashley needn't have worried about anything. Biddy and her team of stalwarts from the WI had everything under control. She had the feeling they could serve up tea, sandwiches and cake for a couple of hundred people in their sleep. The central part of the café floor had been cleared. Chairs had been pushed to the walls so whoever wanted to could sit down. Two enormous brown Betty teapots stood to attention in front of an urn hissing steam on one table. A buffet of freshly made finger sandwiches and tempting fairy cakes, on pretty floral stands, was stretched along several others.

Biddy had already told her off about calling them cupcakes. 'They were fairy cakes in my day and I still make them exactly the same, so fairy cakes they'll always be,' she'd boomed. Ashley didn't dare argue. Instead, biting down a giggle, she turned away and admired the enormous white ceramic bust of Churchill which was a new addition to the café. Petra was certainly embracing all things wartime.

Andrea, cup of tea in hand, came up to her. 'Ashley, come and have a look at this.' She led her over to the far wall of the café. It usually boasted a mural Ashley knew had been painted by Ken, but it was now covered by three freestanding displays. 'We've put up photographs of Jimmy's life on two of them, as you suggested,' the older woman explained. 'And on the third, I thought we could get people to write messages of how they knew Jimmy or why they wanted to come to the funeral.'

'It's a marvellous idea, Andrea,' Ashley said, impressed. 'Thank you.'

'Well, not too original. We try to do it for some of our other guests. Especially the ones who don't have much of a family. I always think it helps to make people see the departed as a proper person, not just an old wrinkled octogenarian sitting in a chair.'

'Absolutely.'

'I love the picture in the middle. It's the one I showed you at that first meeting. Taken not long after the war finished – he was about to start his job at the council. Funny to think his entire life was working for Berecombe

Town Council. People don't have jobs like that nowadays, do they? My niece has had four already and she's only thirty-two.'

Ashley moved closer to the display board. 'Hello again, Jimmy,' she said softly. 'I hope you think we've done you proud.'

Andrea moved closer too and peered at the photograph. She squeezed Ashley's shoulder. 'Oh yes, I think you did.' She gave a huge sigh. 'He'll be missed.' A voice called her and she added, 'I'll leave you to it,' and disappeared.

Reaching out, Ashley touched the photograph gently, tears brimming. 'Oh Jimmy.' Despite the ravages of the scar, Jimmy had appealing looks. He couldn't be called handsome but there was an impishness in the eyes, and his mouth, despite being dragged down at one corner by his disfigurement, curled up at the other as if in readiness for the next joke. 'I wish I'd met you, Jimmy Larcombe,' she whispered. She moved on to the next board to see a picture of Jimmy as an old man. It must have been taken at the care home, as he was sitting in a wheelchair, his knees covered by a rug. The scar was still there but so was the zest for life – and the crooked grin. Ashley could well believe Andrea's claim that he had been popular with the lady residents. 'You go, Jimmy.' She giggled a little. 'Causing hearts to break until the very end.'

'What's that you say? Breaking hearts? Oh yes, that was Jimmy.'

Ashley hadn't been aware of Ruby coming to stand next to her.

'These are bringing back a few memories an' all,' Ruby said. With a wavering finger she pointed at one of Jimmy in uniform. 'That's him just before he went off to war. Looked lovely in a uniform, he did. Joined up not long before that first Christmas. Wanted the Royal Navy but, in their wisdom, they put him in the bloomin' Army. At least it was the Dorsets, he said. At least it was a local lot.' She peered beadily up at Ashley. 'You want to know about the war? Jimmy's war?'

'It would be great, but only when you're ready.'

Ruby cackled. 'When you get to my age, dearie, you grab your chances when you can. No point putting things off.'

'Well, if you're sure.' Ashley thought back to how frail the old woman had looked in church earlier. 'And if you're up to it?'

''Course I'm up to it, child. Now I've said my goodbyes to Jimmy. Go and get me a fresh cuppa and a few sarnies, and I'll be all set.'

# Chapter Twenty-Two

Ashley tracked down Noah talking to the handsome RNLI crew member who had been interviewed earlier. 'This is Oliver,' Noah said. 'He's Emma Tizzard's fiancé. You know, Ken Tizzard is her uncle.'

'Hello Oliver. I keep meaning to pop into the Arts Centre but somehow I always run out of time.'

'No problem,' he replied affably. 'It'll be there another day. Don't think Ken's going anywhere.'

'Just as well.' Ashley pulled a face. 'It's been non-stop since I've been in Berecombe. Speaking of which, Noah, could I borrow the recorder if you've got it on you? Ruby's in the mood for some memory sharing.'

'I heard about your project,' Oliver put in, a lock of black hair falling over his eyes attractively. 'It's a great idea. There'll be volunteer crew who can talk to you about some of the shouts we've been on. There was a dramatic one back in the 70s where they rescued some kids kayaking in the harbour mouth. Got into a bit of trouble and got cold in the water. It was all touch and go for a while. Paul Cash's dad was crew back then. He'll be able to help. You'll find Paul at the police station most days. He's our local policeman.'

'That would be fabulous,' Noah said, his eyes gleaming. He handed over the recorder, adding, 'Could you put Mr Cash on the list of interviewees, Ash?'

'Happy to once I've got time,' Ashley replied, between gritted teeth. Really, Noah could be infuriating sometimes. She began to say, 'What did your last minion die of?' but stopped herself. Didn't seem the thing to say at a wake. She contented herself with, 'I'll be off then. Nice to meet you, Oliver.'

Spotting Eddie head and shoulders above the crowd, which had now gathered in the café, she went over to him. 'I'm going to record some of Ruby's war memories. Fancy sitting in?'

'Sure.' Then he grimaced. 'Noisy in here. You won't record anything great with this amount of background noise. Why not go outside? It's warm enough now.'

'Good idea. Could you grab some food and more tea? Ruby would like some.'

'Yup. I'll meet you guys out there.'

Ashley settled Ruby in a sheltered sunny spot against the wall that separated the café's open space from the beach. Serena followed them but when Ruby flapped her away Ashley was relieved. Ruby's daughter cramped the old lady's style. Luckily, Serena was joined by Peggy and her grandson and disappeared back into the café.

Ruby watched her go with narrowed eyes. 'Called her Serena 'cos I hoped she'd bring me some serenity in life.' She blew out a cackle. 'Not much serene about her, though. Always fussing and faddling.'

Ashley sat on a bench next to Ruby and leaned against the wall. It had soaked up the sun and was blissfully warm on her back. 'It's because she loves you. My parents are the same. Over-protective to an annoying extent.' She gave Ruby a brief smile. 'That's why I escaped down here. To get away from their well-meaning but overbearing attentions.'

'This after your accident? Biddy told me about it.'

Ashley braced herself. She didn't want to talk about that today. 'Yes,' she answered repressively and was relieved to see Eddie appear just then, carrying a laden tray.

He brought an astounding amount of food, plus a whole pot of tea and three mugs. 'Thought you might be hungry.' Setting the tray down, he said, 'There's tuna mayo, cheese and pickle, smoked salmon and cream cheese and, my favourite, cucumber! And a selection of cupcakes to follow.'

'Don't let Biddy hear you call them that,' Ashley reproved. 'Think it's a hanging offence. They're fairy cakes.'

'Quite right too,' Ruby said, eyeing Eddie with suspicion. 'You're very large, aren't you? Are all you Americans big?'

He sat down on a slight wooden chair, making it creak. 'Guess so.' He grinned affably, not taking offence. 'Known many Americans, Mrs Daniels?'

She looked shifty. 'Might have done. At least you were on time with my food. You lot were late to the show in both World Wars.'

'Right,' Ashley intervened, before the old woman could cause any more trouble. 'Shall we have something to eat and a cup of tea and then, if you want, you can tell us more about the war?' Discreetly, she switched on the recorder, not comfortable with the interrogative approach. She wanted to get Ruby to relax and open up. She divided up a few sandwiches while Eddie poured the tea, the pink spotted pot looking incongruous in his big hand.

Ruby nibbled on a cucumber sandwich. 'Lovely,' she said with relish. 'That Petra can put on a good tea, that's for sure. Auntie Florrie made a good tea, even in the war with the rationing. She used to be asked to make the sarnies. Was famous for cutting the bread so thin, it was transparent. No mean feat what with that horrible national loaf we had to suffer. Made it go a long way, you see.'

'And that's who you stayed with in Berecombe, isn't it?' Ruby asked.

'That's right. I went to school for a bit but I didn't like it. The local kids didn't take to us at first. Used to throw stones and call us names. They'd wait at the gate at the end of the school day and lay siege. Soon stopped though. The London kids were tough, you see. They'd square up. Novelty wore off soon enough. I helped Auntie Florrie in the shop when I could. When I left school, I did it as a proper job.'

'Oh yes, you mentioned when we last spoke that they had a shop.' Ashley picked up a salmon and cream cheese finger sandwich and ate it. It was delicious.

'Grocer's. In the high street next to the baker's, with a flat above it. Nice, it was. Auntie Florrie was glad of the help. She'd been running it with only Jimmy since Uncle John died.'

'How did John die?' Eddie asked.

'He got a touch of gas in the last lot. Affected his lungs. He went in…' Ruby paused, screwing up her face, trying to remember. 'No, it's gone. He'd not been around for a good long while when I showed up. What with Jimmy gone to be a soldier, me and Florrie were kept busy. I liked it. Got to know all the folk in the town.' She giggled girlishly. 'Got to know the gossip.'

'What other shops were there, Mrs Daniels?'

'Oh, love,' Ruby cried, putting her hand on Ashley's. 'Get on with you. You can call me Ruby.'

Ashley smiled and pushed the plate of sandwiches nearer. 'Have another, Ruby. The salmon and cream cheese are good.'

'Don't mind if I do.' Ruby took another sandwich and bit into it. 'You're right, it is tasty.' She laughed. 'If you told young Ruby Harris, aged thirteen, working in Larcombe's the Grocer's, taking grief 'cos we was out of Rinso again, that she'd be sitting in some la-di-da place like this eating salmon and cream cheese finger sandwiches, she'd say it was science fiction. Although, now I come to think of it, there was a teashop down here during the war. Not like this one, though. A pot of tea and a carrot scone was the best you could get.'

Ashley was intrigued at the mention of a wartime café and was about to ask about it when Ruby got distracted.

'Those smart phone things!' She gestured with her

sandwich at Eddie's phone lying on the table. 'Our Serena's got one. Works by magic, I reckon.'

'Think you're right there, Mrs Daniels,' Eddie said. 'I haven't a clue how they work either. Only know my life is ruled by the damned thing.'

'Suppose you can call me Ruby too, young man,' the old woman said, her mouth pursing, causing long lines of wrinkles to rivulet up to her nose. 'Seeing as you brought me cake.'

'My pleasure, ma'am.' Eddie nodded gracefully.

Ruby squealed. 'That takes me back, that does. He used to call Florrie "ma'am". Tickled me then and it tickles me now.'

There was a very still pause, then Eddie said, 'You've said that once before. Who was the man who called your aunt ma'am?'

Ruby winked. 'Wouldn't you like to know. That'll save for another day.' She turned to Ashley. 'You wanted to know about Jimmy in the war, didn't you, lovie? Got your recorder thingy set up?'

Ashley sensed Eddie's frustration but moved the little handheld device nearer Ruby. 'It's all ready to go. Tell us. In your own words and in your own time.'

## Chapter Twenty-Three

Ruby drank some tea, wiped the corners of her mouth with her handkerchief and began speaking. 'When Jimmy and the doctor picked me up I didn't realize Jimmy had already enlisted. He was waiting to find out where he was going to be sent for training. I was too excited being in a car for the first time. Been on plenty of buses and trams and the odd train or two, but not a car. It was a grand old car too. I can still smell the leather of the upholstery all mixed up with the doctor's pipe baccy.

'Jimmy left soon afterwards for training. Near broke Florrie's heart. She'd lost her John to one war, or as good as, and didn't want to lose her son. She began to rely on me a lot. Said I was the daughter she'd never had. Showed me how to put on my lippy just so. "You've got to wear your red badge of courage," she used to say. We had some right laughs together. And then she drank a bit more of Reg's blackberry gin and got a bit more drunk and a bit more giggly, and then I'd put her to bed.

'We found out Jimmy had gone in the 2nd Dorsets. Next letter we had, he was in Belgium. Made me laugh sometimes. Here was me mam, shipping me off down here and right in the path of the Germans if they ever decided to invade, when there was nothing going on in London! The Phoney War, they called it. No bombs, no gas, just a lot of waiting around for it to start. It was almost a relief when it did. The Germans slunk into Belgium, right where Jimmy and his lot were. He said later they'd had leaflets dropped on them. Can you believe that – a leaflet! Told them they was surrounded and to surrender. That the Germans treated their prisoners well. I won't repeat what Jimmy said about *that*, but I'd never heard a boy swear so much.'

'He got out okay, then?' Eddie asked.

'Oh he did, eventually. Headed, along with the rest of the BEF, to Dunkirk. Five days and five nights of marching and fighting, it took the Dorsets. They got picked up by a Thames dredger off the Mole at what was left of the harbour. There they was, queuing to get on, and all the time the bastard Germans were machine-gunning them from their *Stukas* above.' Ruby shook her head. 'I didn't know Jimmy very well before he went to war, but even I could tell he'd changed when he got back to us. Dunkirk! We nearly lost the war before it had begun. And would have lost it, if we hadn't got our boys out. And then we were alone.' She tutted. 'That was when the invasion felt like it was about to happen, especially down here, especially when the Channel Islands went under.' She shuddered. 'That was a bad day.'

'Is that how Jimmy was injured? At Dunkirk?' Ashley asked, gently.

Ruby nodded. 'He never told us exactly how it happened but he got burned bad. The scarring didn't heal well on his arm and it stopped a bit of movement. He'd jumped in the water, you see, to fish someone out. Drowning he was, Jimmy said. Young kid of eighteen. Jimmy stayed in the water with him until they got on the boat. That was Jimmy's war finished. Frustrated him it did, when he came back to Berecombe and saw the younger boys going off to fight. Florrie was pleased though, to have her boy back, and when the rationing came in we needed all the help we could get in the shop. Rationing made extra work.' She stopped and drank some more tea. *'The cup that cheers but never inebriates.'* She smiled. 'That's what they used to say. Mind you, when it was on the ration, we squeezed every last ounce of flavour out of a potful. Waste not, want not. The shop's still there, by the way. In the high street. Well, the building is, with the flat above. Had a fine sea view over the bay, I seem to remember. Serena drove me past. Looks like it's some kind of art gallery thing now. Florrie will be turning in her grave.'

Ashley made a memo to herself to photograph it. She thought she knew the building Ruby was referring to. 'Something Peggy said in church,' she said. 'About her father Reg. He went off the sea after Dunkirk. Was he a soldier too?'

'Oh no, dearie. He took his little fishing boat off to see if it was needed.'

'Needed for what?'

'To evacuate the men,' Eddie put in. 'Is that right, Ruby? They were called the Little Ships.'

'The Miracle of Dunkirk,' Ruby added. 'That's what they called it. They needed small boats to get right into shore, you see. They put out an appeal on the radio for boats to get to Dover and Ramsgate and then over to France. After a few days of the Germans bombing it, there was precious little left of Dunkirk harbour, so they took the men off the beach. Reg got drunk one night, a few months after he got back. He started to talk. Poor Florrie was beside herself. We'd just had a letter from Jimmy to say he was in a hospital Kent way and had to stay there for a bit because of his injuries. We didn't really know what had happened to him but after Reg finished talking we were in the picture.

'Reg took his little boat, *The Skylark*, round to Poole to see if he could help. He knew Jimmy was somewhere out there, see, and he wanted to do his bit. Get the lad back.' Ruby sniffed. 'Funny thing was, they turned *The Skylark* down. Said there wasn't enough room on her. He cadged a lift with a mate and they took a pleasure craft over. Said it was like going into hell. The first they could see was black plumes of smoke coming off the sea. That's when they knew they were near.' She swallowed. 'Then they went in nearer the beach and all they could see was lines of men, standing in the water, in the sea, holding their rifles on their shoulders. They got as many on board as they could and one said he'd been in the water for ten hours. Ten hours! And each time Reg went back he thought it might be Jimmy he picked out of the water, half-drowned, half-mad, shot to pieces.'

'Oh my God.' Ashley put her hand to her throat.

'Don't think God had much to do with that day,' Ruby said drily. 'Reg said he went back and forth on that boat for five days solid, getting the boys out. Said the boat next to them got a direct hit.'

'What do you mean?'

'The Germans. The bloody *Luftwaffe*! They were

strafing the sea, machine-gunning men drowning in the water, climbing onto the boats, trying to escape. Reg said when a *Stuka* came at you from out of the sky it was like it went right down the back of your neck. It was the howling noise it made, you see. Those poor boys, some of them just sitting on the beach, waiting for a boat to get them out.' Ruby dabbed at her eyes. 'Sitting ducks.'

Ashley put a hand on the old lady's arm. 'Don't say any more if it upsets you.'

'I'm not upset. I'm bloody angry! Bloody Jerries!'

'Did Reg ever come across Jimmy?'

Ruby shook her head. 'No. None of us knew what had happened to him until we got the letter from the hospital. I suppose Reg felt he could tell us what it was like then, once we knew Jimmy had got out.'

Eddie sat back. 'Jeez. No wonder Reg didn't like the sea after that. What a hellish experience.'

'Well, he went back to his fishing but there wasn't a lot to be done. Had to watch out for the mines in the bay. That was the end for many a fisherman who didn't look out. Florrie used to write to me for a bit, after I went home. She told me he was never the same. Didn't want anything to do with anything that reminded him of the war, including Jimmy. After the war, Reg married a girl who had family up north and decided that was that.

Peggy's just told me he never went to sea again. Never even went for a stroll by the beach.'

'And Jimmy came back to you,' Ashley asked. 'Once he was better?'

'Oh yes. Jimmy came back to us,' Ruby said with a gleam in her eye. 'And that's when the fun really began.'

## Chapter Twenty-Four

Serena marched over to them. 'Mother, I insist you stop all this nonsense. You're worn out!'

Ashley switched off the recorder. 'Oh, but Ruby was just about to tell us about Jimmy and when he came home from the war.'

Serena ignored her. Forcefully helping her mother to her feet, she said, 'Look at you. As white as a sheet. And sitting out here in this cold wind. Come on, back to the bed and breakfast with you. A nice little nap and then we'll find somewhere for dinner.'

Ruby was swept off before either Ashley or Eddie could do anything about it.

Eddie pulled a face. 'That was frustrating. I thought we were gonna get something more out of Ruby about

Jimmy.' He picked up a sandwich and ate it whole. 'And I'm sure she's holding out on us about the Americans.'

'I think so too. We got some fabulous stuff though, didn't we? It's the way Ruby talks. You can imagine yourself there. Sitting in the back room, waiting for news of someone at war, getting his letters and reading between the lines. Listening to a traumatized man tell of the hell he went through in order to pull men out of the sea, and all the time expecting to find his nephew.'

'It's fascinating. Don't know why Ruby's daughter is so anti her mother sharing her memories.'

'Over-protective, I suppose. And Ruby did look tired. It's been an emotional day for her. Maybe it was enough for one session.' She shot Eddie an anxious look. 'It's not cold out here, is it? I thought it was sheltered against the wall and in the sun.'

'No, it's fine. I think Ruby would have told us if she'd been cold.'

Ashley gave a short laugh. 'That's true. She doesn't hold back. What a time to live through, though. I can't imagine it. Food rationed, loved ones at war, the fear of being invaded by the enemy. And that was right at the start of the war. They had another five years to get through.'

'And it's true what Ruby said. Dunkirk changed the course of the war. They got the best part of the British army out of France that day. If they hadn't, well, the war might have been a lot shorter but it could have had a very different result.'

'And it all seems so long ago, and yet Ruby could easily be my great-grandmother. I can't believe it happened to people we can talk to.' Ashley stared out at the sea, a dreamy blue vastness stretching serenely out to a pale sky. The land that had been so bitterly fought over was only twenty or thirty miles away. The Channel Islands a short ferry ride. The same islands which had been invaded by the enemy. She suppressed a shiver; she could all too easily imagine a German warship appearing on the horizon. She felt Eddie scrutinizing her closely.

'You okay?'

She only had time to nod briefly before mourners began to spill out of the café. A rhythmic jingling of bells sounded, punctuated by the sharp yap of Biddy's poodle. The dog hardly ever barked, so Ashley looked over. 'Oh, it's the Morris dancers,' she cried. 'Of course!' In a blink all her introspective dwelling on World War Two fled.

'Morris dancers, oh boy!' Eddie's mouth dropped open. 'I haven't seen any since I got here.'

Ashley got to her feet, wincing slightly at her stiffness. 'I told you it was going to be a unique funeral. According to Andrea, Jimmy was a keen folk music fan.

Let's go over there,' she said, pointing to the far side of the space by the bookshop. 'We'll get a better view.'

'I've got an idea. You get on the wall and hang onto me. I can see over people's heads anywhere I stand.'

Ashley looked at the wall doubtfully. 'I'll never be able to get up there.'

'Ah, come on kiddo, where's your Dunkirk spirit?' Taking off his suit jacket, he unbuttoned his shirt and loosened his tie. 'Get onto the bench first and then hop on. Come on, I'll help.'

Before she could think up an argument, Ashley found herself gripped around the waist by two strong hands and propelled onto the bench. Then Eddie held her hand in a tight grip while she stepped onto the wall. The sense of achievement was dizzying. She hadn't done anything quite so physically adventurous since before the accident. And, while she was sure it may seem trivial to some people, being able to climb on top of a wall, like any other thirty-something, felt exhilarating. Eddie turned his back to her but kept her hands in his. He leaned back against her so she had support. His shoulders felt very warm against her legs and his subtle scent drifted up to her. She wobbled a little and Eddie's grip tightened.

Petra and Noah helped clear some tables and chairs to make a space and the dancers formed a figure of six. Their white shirts and trousers, which gleamed in the warm spring sunshine, were set off with red waistcoats and tricorn hats from which sprouted a selection of feathers. They gripped long sticks and an accordionist stood ready to play.

One of the men held up his stick. 'This one's for Jimmy,' he yelled, in a rich Devon accent. 'Rest in peace, old man, and may you dance up a storm wherever you've ended up. Ready, lads? Dick's Maggot!' He assumed his position and the accordionist struck a note. Ashley had seen lots of Morris dancing in Ludlow so knew what to expect. She rarely gave it much thought but seeing it anew through Eddie's eyes, she wondered, with a giggle, what he was making of it. Then she remembered him saying his hobby was folklore, so he was probably lapping it up.

The dancers performed twice, once with their sticks, which they thwacked against one another's with terrifying ferocity. Along with their wild cries and the clatter of their boots on the concrete, it was a stirring spectacle. Certainly little Elvis, Biddy's deaf assistance dog, thought so. He became so agitated, Biddy had to take him back inside the café. With a final coming together of the sticks, the dancers yelled, 'Huzzah!', scattering seagulls who flew cackling into the sky, and then all was still again.

Eddie slid round to face Ashley. He reached up, took

her by the waist and lifted her down. She slid down against his warm cotton-shirted chest and over his firm thighs. Her woollen dress caught, embarrassingly, on the buckle of his belt and Eddie held her close while he untangled her, his hand hot on her stomach. Again, she could feel his heart pounding through the thin material of his shirt, feel his arousal, smell his intoxicating maleness, sandalwood and warm man. Goodness knows what she smelled of. The dress, so welcome first thing in the morning and in the dead cold of the church, was now, in the balmy March sunshine, becoming uncomfortably hot.

'There, all sorted,' he said but didn't release her. Instead he gazed into her eyes intently. 'That was a thrill, wasn't it?'

'The dancing?' Ashley decided to play it safe.

'Yeah, sure.' He gave a crooked grin, playing along. 'The dancing. Some say it all began as an ancient springtime fertility ritual with the Druids. Banish the darkness of the winter, bless the land, ensure fecundity of the soil and the potency of the body.'

Ashley's breath left her. 'Oh,' she croaked. She could stay like this forever, with his strong arms hot against her back, her breasts pressed into him. So close, she could see the flecks of green in his intense, hazel eyes. Feel his warm breath whispering on her skin.

'Ashley, I know this isn't the time, but—'

Eddie got no further, as Noah suddenly bounced up to them. 'Hey Ed, after the men have had a cuppa they're willing to take a few of us through the moves. Do you fancy it?' He looked curiously from Eddie to Ashley. 'Go on, be a sport. It'll be a laugh.'

There were many times in Ashley's long acquaintance with her cousin when she had had reason to throttle him. This was one. It was just as well the Morris dancers' sticks weren't within reach.

Eddie released her, a regretful expression on his face. 'Not the time or place,' he murmured. 'Again.'

She watched as Noah took Eddie's arm and dragged him off. In frustration, she whispered, 'It never is!'

As Noah introduced Eddie to the dancers, Ashley was left standing alone. She sank back onto the bench. Proximity to Eddie had an alarming effect on her and she wasn't sure what to do about it. One thing was certain, she had little idea how he really felt about her. And Noah had possibly just robbed her of an opportunity to find out.

## Chapter Twenty-Five

The mourners gradually drifted away. Peggy and her family came to bid Ashley goodbye, thanking her profusely for giving them the chance to attend, and then left. Ashley sat on the bench in the sunshine. Now it was all over, she was exhausted. But it was a good sort of tiredness. The sort that came with having done a job well. From the café she could hear the clattering of plates and Biddy bossing the WI women as they cleared up. In the space in front, the Morris men were attempting to teach some hardy volunteers a few moves. Eddie was wielding a stick. His shoulder muscles bunched under the thin shirt in a way that had lust curling hotly inside her again. Noah was trying, and failing, to master the curious half-skip, half-jump that the dancers had made look effortless.

'Penny for them?' It was Petra, looking as immaculate

as ever, her bright-red lipstick the only colour vivid against the black and white outfit. She had Elvis on a lead and sat down on the bench. The little dog jumped up onto her lap and she petted him absent-mindedly. 'Cool having someone else do the cleaning up for a change. Biddy's doing a great job in there. Nothing for me to do. Got sent out as I was in the way, apparently.'

Ashley dragged her thoughts away from Eddie with difficulty. 'She put you in charge of Elvis, so you're obviously a trusted ally. He's very co-ordinated with your outfit.'

'He is, isn't he? I like poodles. They don't shed and he's a cutie. I'd love a dog but I just don't have the time. Full-time job, dogs are.' Petra spread out her full skirts, revealing a mass of net petticoat underneath.

'I do admire your style,' Ashley said, eyeing the brilliantly white petticoat. 'It's very definite isn't it, very thought out.'

'Thanks. Sort of goes with the territory.'

'What do you mean?'

'I'm in a singing group. It's a trio. Close harmony. Think the Andrews Sisters or the Puppini Sisters. Have you heard of them?'

Ashley nodded.

'We specialize in songs from the 40s and 50s. Only I like the costumes so much, they've overlapped into real life. We wear 40s-inspired uniforms for the wartime stuff but I love these 50s-style dresses. All the nipped-in waists and full skirts. They used to use a sugar solution to starch these types of petticoats, did you know? Thank God I can use a modern equivalent. I hate wasps!'

Ashley laughed. She was beginning to really like Petra. 'I didn't. Not a lot of sugar around in the war, so one reason for a different silhouette, I suppose.'

'Not a lot of anything during the war, let alone dress material. That's why the skirts were narrow and knee-length. I think, maybe, that's why the songs are so important. Makes up for the dullness in life. No fripperies, make-up hard to get hold of and, of course, you were living on your emotions all the time. I love the 50s clothes but I adore singing the songs from the war.'

'So you do the singing along with managing the café?'

'Yes.'

'No wonder you don't have time for a dog.'

Petra laughed. 'I hear you, girl. Life gets good when I merge the two. We've put on one or two shows in the café when I've opened it up for evening meals.'

'I hope you drew the line at wartime food.'

Petra laughed again. 'Well, some of it isn't too bad. You ever tried Lord Woolton's Pie? Vegetables in a Marmite gravy, pastry lid with a teensy grating of cheese on top, and porridge oats to bulk it out.'

'No I haven't, and you're not selling it to me.'

'Doctor Carrot and Potato Pete would be deeply disappointed.'

'Doctor who?'

'Not Doctor Who,' Petra said, eyes brimming with mirth. 'They were two cartoon characters used to encourage people to eat more vegetables during the war. Ruby will know all about them.'

'Okay. I'm still not sure about that pie, though.' Ashley pulled a face.

'Maybe I won't put it on the café menu, then.' Petra stretched back and put her elbows on the table behind her. She stared at Noah who was trying to flick a handkerchief, and then narrowed her eyes as she watched Eddie. 'You were miles away when I sat down. Your hot American catches the eye, doesn't he?'

Ashley followed her look. Eddie was bending over, out of breath, hands on knees, suit trousers stretched snugly over his behind. 'He does, but you're wrong about him being my American.'

'Oh?' Petra said, interested. 'Could have fooled me with the way he was eating you up with his eyes earlier on.'

Ashley sighed. 'I'm not saying I'm not attracted, but I don't know anything about him.'

'With some men that's the best way,' Petra cackled.

'He's keen though, I reckon. And he seems a decent sort of bloke. You don't find many of those around.'

'True.' Noah tried a complicated step and fell hard. He lay sprawled on his back laughing uproariously. To change the subject, Ashley said, 'It might not be the best time to mention this, seeing as he's just fallen flat on his backside, but I think Noah's interested in you, you know. And he's another of the good guys. I've known him all my life, so I can vouch for him.'

Petra glanced at her. 'I like him too but wasn't sure how he felt about me. He's always so friendly. To *everyone.*'

'That's Noah. Like a big puppy dog.' As he rolled around the floor, giggling helplessly, she added, 'As you can see.' They erupted into laughter. 'He loves everyone, that's true, but I think he likes you quite a lot. I can tell.'

'You two close then?'

'Very.'

'That's nice. I haven't got anyone like that.'

Petra's voice was wistful and Ashley was just about to ask her more when she caught sight of Chloe Deverell, the cameraman and Keeley Sharma emerging from the café. 'Hide me,' she squeaked and ducked down until they'd gone.

Petra looked around. She sniggered. 'What have you done, to have to hide from the press? And Keeley wrote such a nice article about us all. It's all right. They've got into their cars now.'

Ashley sat back up. 'It's not Keeley, it's Chloe Deverell. She's the woman from hell.'

'Oh,' Petra said, sounding disappointed. 'And she comes across as so nice and friendly on the telly. So, girl, what are you going to do about Eddie?'

Ashley bit her lip and frowned. 'Nothing. He's only here on a temporary contract with the university, from what I can gather. He'll be back off to the States at some point.' She had a flashback to the kiss and regret curled in her stomach.

'Why get heavy about it? Have a quick fling. Live in the moment. Enjoy your handsome American while you can.'

Ashley looked over to her. Screwing up her face, she said, 'Not really my style. I'm one of those horrible falls-deeply-in-love-quickly sort of girl.'

'Fair enough. You know anything about his love life? A man as good-looking as that doesn't come without some kind of history.'

Ashley thought back to the evening in her flat. 'He mentioned briefly getting his heart broken. Maybe he's in no hurry to get involved again?'

'Oh!' Petra clasped her hands to her heart and tilted her head, batting her lashes. 'How could you resist a broken-hearted man? Maybe that's why he left the States?'

'Maybe.'

Petra jumped up suddenly. Waving to a Keira Knightley lookalike materializing from the café, she pulled Ashley to her feet. 'There's Millie. My boss. Come on, do you want to meet her? The girl's a legend in this town.'

Millie, friendly and obviously pregnant, took her hands. 'Ashley,' she said warmly. 'How great to meet you. You've done a fabulous job; Biddy was singing your praises in there.' She rolled her eyes. 'And Biddy doesn't do that very often.'

'Then I'm very honoured. Thank you for loaning us the café.'

'It was the very least I could do. Ah, here comes Ken. I think you two have already met?'

'We have.' Ashley turned to him. 'Hi, Ken.'

'Hello there, my friend. You given up on me?'

'What do you mean?'

'You were going to come by the workshop.'

Ashley gasped. 'I was. I'm so sorry, Ken, I haven't had a moment.'

'No worries. You've been busy getting this organized, I can see, and you've aced it.'

'Aw, thank you. And yes, it's kept me busy. I promise to come and see you, though. Soon.'

'I'll hold you to that. I've got a proposition for you. Now, I'm going back in to face Biddy's wrath and mop up some of those scones that are left over. No point leaving food to go to waste.'

'No chance of that happening when you're around,' Millie said fondly.

'Aw, come on, Mil. I've got three growing boys at home. I never get the chance to eat. They go through cupboards like dinosaurs on heat. I haven't come close to as much as a ready salted crisp ever since our Sean was weaned.'

'Go on,' she said, with a little push. 'Go in with Petra – she's put a plate aside for you.' Anticipating his next question, she added, 'And no, I won't tell Tess.'

'The woman's always got me on a diet,' he grumbled. 'You come and see me, Ashley. Right then, Petra, show me the grub.' With a wave, he followed Petra into the café.

'That was all very intriguing.' Millie turned to Ashley, her dark eyes sparkling with humour. 'Do I have to tell my best friend Tess that her husband is making propositions to other women?'

'God, no. I am, or rather *was*, an art teacher. I

promised to go and see Ken but I just haven't had the time.'

'Well, I know he was looking for someone to help with the paperwork.' Millie pulled a face. 'Not Ken's strong point.' She put her head on one side, her thick, dark hair swinging. 'Are you looking for a job?'

'No. Yes. Maybe.' Ashley laughed. 'Not making myself very clear, am I? I'm not sure what I'm looking for. A change of lifestyle, I think.'

'In that case, Berecombe's an excellent place to be.' She smiled. 'What do you think you'll do, now the funeral is over?'

'I'll help Biddy with the parade and the tea party if she'll let me, and I'm helping Noah with the museum project. He's got me taking photographs. I suppose I should have taken some today but it didn't seem the thing to do.'

Millie pulled a face and then laughed. 'Not really, no.'

Ashley looked over to where the Morris dancers were now wandering off to The Old Harbour for a well-earned pint. 'I'd love to get some shots of the dancers.'

'Oh, they'll be around for most of the summer. You'll have a chance to catch them again.'

Millie went on to say something else but Ashley didn't hear. She was distracted by the sight of Eddie taking a call on his mobile. He was thrusting a hand through his hair and speaking urgently.

'Who will be around again?' Noah bounced up and slung a casual arm around Ashley. 'Hi, Millie. Good to see you again. Is your esteemed brother-in-law around, by any chance? I need to catch him to talk through plans for the dinner dance at his hotel.' He loosened his tie and tugged open his shirt, running a hand over his brow. 'Oh lordy, you have to be fit to Morris dance. I had no idea!'

'Come into the café,' Millie said, indulgently. 'I'll get you some homemade ginger beer. With lots of ice. And maybe a slice of cider cake? As for Alex, he'll be up at The Henville, I expect.' As they went into the café Ashley could hear her saying how much she was looking forward to the black-tie event.

She turned to face Eddie. He was standing, hands on lean hips, staring at the ground, deep in thought. Going up to him, she asked, 'Anything wrong?'

'Oh, Ashley.' He looked up, a frown creasing his face, obviously still preoccupied. 'Yeah,' he said on a long breath. 'Phone call from home. Mom's not well again. I need to get back. Got some time owing for Easter, so I guess I'll use that. Shame, though. I was looking forward to the arrival of the GIs and the parade.'

'Do you think you'll be back in time for the dance? At The Henville?' Ashley blurted it out. Until that second she hadn't realized how much she wanted to go. To dress up in something gorgeous, get her hair done, put on some make-up. Dance with him. She gulped. 'Sorry. That was amazingly insensitive.'

'No, it's okay. Got to come back for my job, so yes, I hope so. Depends though, on how sick Mom is.'

'Of course. We'll see you when we see you, then. We'll miss you.'

'Will you? Will you miss me, Ashley?'

Ashley stared hard at the sandy concrete beneath her feet. She couldn't believe how tactless she'd been. Banging on about a dinner dance when he'd just heard his mum was poorly! Ridiculous tears, tiredness from the day no doubt, made her eyes hot. 'Yes, I'll miss you,' she whispered. 'You know how much.' But when she looked up again, Eddie had gone.

## Chapter Twenty-Six

Ashley threw herself into Berecombe community life with ferocity. Biddy welcomed her input with organising the parade and the tea party which would follow, although there was very little left to do. She picked up her painting again and resumed her early morning rambles around the town taking photographs. It was to her surprise that she came back to the little flat one day to find her walking stick abandoned on the sofa. Thinking back, she hadn't used it for days.

She and Noah relaxed over the Easter Bank Holiday and ate and drank too much. He drove her to the designer outlet at Street and she bought a long silver-grey dress for the dinner dance. She also booked in with the alarmingly named Klassy Kutz to have her hair dressed on the day. She did it all feeling slightly numb;

there seemed little point in going unless Eddie was there. And then she chided herself for being so feeble and tried to be more enthusiastic for Noah's sake. Neither of them heard anything from Eddie. Ashley told herself there would be no reason to; they were just friends, after all, but she admitted to disappointment. Noah said nothing on the matter.

The day of the parade and party dawned bright and clear. It was, thankfully, going to be a warm April day. Ashley secured her place on some steps slightly above the promenade at the town end. It would give her a good vantage point from which to take photographs. As she watched the seven veterans who had made it back to Berecombe parade past, emotion blocked her throat. Hollow shells of their former selves but stiff-backed and proud, they each wore a cap emblazoned with *WWII* and a khaki blouson jacket pinned with medals and the Stars and Stripes flag. Four were pushed in wheelchairs but the other three men marched, muscle memory and sheer stubbornness providing the age-old rhythm. She remembered, just in time, to take some photos but was unable to see the viewfinder through tears. They were followed by their families, the Sea Cadets and Scouts, and various dignitaries all heading to the square outside the theatre where long trestle tables had been set up for the tea party.

Biddy, looking important in an emerald-green suit and matching hat, went past, holding the arm of her councillor husband. She waved, queen-like. As Ashley joined the crowds following on behind, she was passed by those walking more quickly. Many greeted her by name. Emotion choked her once again. It had been good to be part of the school community but Berecombe's community was something truly special.

She hung back once she arrived, to appreciate the sight. The cobbled square was surrounded on three sides by buildings and open on the fourth to the sea. It made a dramatic backdrop. The table of honour, covered with a snowy-white cloth and flowers, was decorated with a mass of red, white and blue bunting. Seven American flags fluttered in the gentle breeze coming off the sea and the guests of honour were already seated. Biddy and her team had done a fantastic job. Once again, the stalwart members of the WI had been called upon to provide refreshments – sandwiches and cake – and a team of local sixth formers, smart in white shirts and black trousers, were doing sterling work pouring tea. Noah, excellent at the big ideas, had come up trumps, but she knew the finer details were down to Biddy. Even the flowers, pretty in bud vases and set in intervals along each table, were in the red, white and blue theme. Over the sound system Vera Lynn sang 'When the Lights Go On Again

All Over the World'. Again, Ashley felt the sting of hot tears.

'Come on, my lovely,' a voice called. 'Come and sit with us.' It was Ken. Ashley slid onto the end of the bench and was introduced to his family: three boys ranging from gangly twenty-something Sean who blushed furiously when she said hi, down to a cheeky teenager and a boy too busy cramming in sandwiches to say anything.

Tess, Ken's wife, passed her a tissue, asking, in a broad Birmingham accent, 'All right, bab? All a bit emotional, this.' She turned to one of her sons. 'Roland,' she scolded the youngest boy, in an abrupt change of tone. 'Will you leave some food for somebody else? And mind your manners and pass the plate of sandwiches. And don't you dare feed the seagulls. Take my advice, my lover,' she added as she rolled her eyes at Ashley, 'give birth to girls!'

The afternoon passed with speeches, both national anthems, tears and much laughter, and then onto the temporary stage put up against the low wall nearest the sea, came three women.

Tess nudged Ashley quite hard. 'The Jenny WRENs, bostin' they are.' When Ashley looked blank, she added, 'It's our Petra. It's her singing group. They don't have a band. They sing archipelago, like.'

'It's acapella, Mum,' said Louis, with all the scorn only a teenaged boy could muster. 'Get it right.'

'All right, Mr Know-It-All,' Tess responded, unfazed. 'Pass them mini sausages and do something useful.'

Ashley looked harder. 'Of course.' Petra, hardly recognizable in an Air Force-blue tightly fitted suit and perky beret, came to the middle microphone and began to sing. 'I didn't know she was going to perform.'

'Last minute thing. Your Noah thought it was a good idea. Looks golden all gussied up, doesn't she?'

Ashley admired Petra, hair done up in an outrageously large victory roll and her lips painted a vibrant red. The pseudo-military uniform revealed no flesh but was deeply sexy in that it clung to every curve. Sheer black stockings helped. 'She does, she really does.' Glancing over at Noah, on the top table, she could see he agreed. She wondered what it would take to get them together.

'Aw, Mum,' moaned Roland. 'Do I have to stay for this? It's boring. Can I go up town now?'

'You can, but you'll have to take one of your brothers with you,' Tess responded tartly.

'It'll have to be Louis then,' Sean said, as he stared at the trio of women on stage. 'I'm staying.'

'Here you go, boys,' Ken reached into his pocket and

pulled out two ten-pound notes. 'Back by six, mind. Now scoot.'

'Thanks, Dad.' Louis's eyes were gleaming. He grabbed a handful of sandwiches and his little brother's hand and left.

'Ah, here's Ruby and Serena,' Ken said as the women made their way over. 'Shuffle up a bit, Tess. They can sit on the end.'

Ruby sat by Ashley, plonking herself down. 'Hello, dearie. I'm going to enjoy this. Wouldn't be able to hear proper back there.'

The Jenny WRENs sang their way through a selection of songs, their voices echoing around the hard stone walls. 'This is the Army Mr Jones' was blasted out, everyone turned into mush with 'I'll Be Seeing You' and 'The White Cliffs of Dover' and then the mood was brought back up with 'Kiss Me Goodnight Sergeant Major' and 'We're Gonna Hang Out the Washing on the Siegfried Line'. Each song was belted out with smiles and dance routines. Ashley was impressed.

When they'd finished, Petra wandered past and Ruby grabbed her hand. 'Oh, that was lovely. You all sang so well. I love the old ones.' She began to sing something jaunty but nonsensical.

'Mum, shush,' Serena said, embarrassed.

Ashley had to agree; she thought Ruby had lost it. She couldn't make out the words at all.

Petra grinned and joined in, the words still unintelligible, but her voice was even more stunning up close.

They laughed as they took in everyone's bemused expressions, then Petra apologized and said she'd been summoned to the top table to say hello to the guests of honour.

Ashley turned to Ruby. 'What was that all about?'

Ruby chuckled. 'It was a nonsense song that was all the rage when I was a kid. "Mairzy Doats", it was called.'

Ashley was nonplussed. 'Mairzy Doats,' she said and then repeated it more slowly. The penny dropped. 'Oh! It's about a horse eating oats!'

'And don't forget the little lambs and all that ivy,' Ruby finished. 'It was a real hit, as the young folk say.'

Ashley didn't think it was what the young folk said at all but didn't like to correct her. She wondered what Louis and Roland would make of a song that sounded like little more than a nursery rhyme; they looked far too sophisticated.

Ruby's face took on a dreamy quality. 'I used to sing it in the shop. Chet said I had a fine voice.'

'Oh, Mother,' Serena butted in with a sigh. 'Please don't start on with all that nonsense again.'

'Ken,' Tess said quickly. 'You know what I fancy, kiddo? A nice big swirly ice-cream from The Icicle Works. Could do with stretching my legs an' all. Come on, Serena,' she said, as she lifted the woman up by the arm. 'I bet you could do with getting away from all this too.'

'Well, I don't know. What about Mother?'

'Ruby will be fine with Ashley,' Tess said, firmly. 'Neither of them are going anywhere. And we'll be back as soon as you know it. Come on, our Sean. You too.' She gave Ashley a broad wink and frog-marched Serena off.

'So, who's Chet, Ruby?' Ashley asked. 'I'd love to know more about him.'

## Chapter Twenty-Seven

'Chet was a GI. Handsome as the sun and twice as dazzling. Dazzled me, anyways.' Ruby glanced across at the table of US veterans. 'He'd be as old as that lot over there now. Nothing like the sight of your own generation to make you realize how old you really are.' She turned back to Ashley, her vivid blue eyes glistening.

Ashley reached a hand over. She held Ruby's tight. It was frail, with the bones of a bird but soft and smooth. 'Age can be a state of mind.'

'You keep believing that, love, and then tell yourself it when you're my age.'

'Sorry.'

'What for, dearie?'

'Patronizing you.'

Ruby squeezed her hand back. 'Stuff and nonsense.'

She blew out a breath and changed the subject. 'Where's your handsome American then?'

'Eddie? He had to go back home. His mum was taken ill.'

'Now, that's a shame. Was quite looking forward to seeing him again. Never hurts to have a good-looking chap to pin your eyes on. And he's a smasher. And don't look at me like that, my girl. I may be old but I can still appreciate a handsome man.'

Ashley didn't want to talk about Eddie. She'd missed him today more than she could imagine. 'Chet, you say he was handsome too?'

'That he was. I'll never forget when they came into town. The Yanks, that is. We'd had enough of the war, you see. Enough of the rations and the death. I'd been working proper in the shop for two years by then. I was just shy of my sixteenth birthday. It wasn't like it is now. All these gappy years and whatnot. You were at school and then you were in work. A grown-up, earning. It was hard work, mind. Folk had got weary by this point. Everything was too hard. Too much of a struggle to feed the family on the scratchings you were allowed. Fed up of the blackout too. Of course we didn't have it as bad down here as they did in London and Coventry, but we got the odd stray bomb out of a plane lost on the way to Plymouth, or a leftover one on the way back. Jerry didn't like wasting no bombs; he dropped the lot, even on somewhere with no docks or factories. One night a house on the front got flattened. You know where I mean? It was where the gardens are now, just behind that posh bookshop in the old seamen's chapel. I see they never built on it. Good thing too. Three people died in that house. The only girl who survived was a friend of mine. She was in service there. Took shelter in a doorway. They used to say it was the strongest part of the house, you see. It was the only bit left standing when the fire service got there. They hauled her out with just a broken arm. Miracle, it was. She went away somewhere afterwards.' Ruby tapped her head. 'Went a bit doolally. Not surprised.' Ruby leaned nearer and dropped her voice. 'Buried, she was, in the rubble, with her dead mistress on top of her. Not nice,' she added, with masterly understatement.

Ashley shuddered. 'I can't imagine what you all had to go through.'

'Let's hope you only have to imagine,' Ruby said, sourly. 'It was bad in the shop too. Long hours, nothing to sell, and what we could sell, we had to eke out into bitty rations. Folk took it out on us. Tempers flared. We were all so tired, you see. Tired of having to cope. When the Yanks came to town, it was like seeing your very first technicolour film. We'd lived in shades of grey for so long – even that national loaf was grey and gritty – and then we had this burst of colour.'

'When did you first become aware of them?'

'It was winter when they came. Not far off Christmas. Another Christmas at war, everyone was saying.' Ruby chuckled. 'Oh yes, everyone was moaning left, right and centre by then. We needed a shot of glamour and, boy, we got it. The black soldiers came first. They set up all the camps for the men on the hill. Whole load of tents and concrete lookouts. Got the officers' quarters ready, the NAAFI. They worked those lads hard. The officers told us not to talk to them. Told us it wasn't allowed for white folk to mix with the "coloureds", as they called them.'

Ashley winced at the term.

'But we weren't having any American swanking it over us, so we took no notice. I served them in the shop and they went in The Old Harbour and tried the beer. No one was telling us what to do! They were such nice, polite lads too. So young. Never been away from home. Florrie and I got right fond of one or two of them.'

'Was Chet a black soldier?'

'No dearie, he came afterwards. I can remember when I met him as clear as day. I was walking up the high street. Florrie had sent me up to the post office. I was hurrying, as it was cold and I'd forgotten my hat. I was out of breath and it was all steaming out. All I could hear was my panting. It was always so quiet, see. No traffic. Only the odd bus. No one except the doctor had petrol for a car, and if they did they got talked about, 'cos we all knew they'd got it on the black market. I was halfway there and heard such a bloomin' racket. What a hullabaloo it was. Jeeps. A whole load of jeeps driving up the street! And, as they passed, all these soldiers were hanging out of the back, waving, smiling, shouting that they'd come to win the war for us. Accents right out of Hollywood, they had. I stood there gawping – must have looked a right sight. They blocked the high street, these jeeps. Someone at the top of the hill had gone the wrong way, so all the others backed up. Quite funny, when you think about it. They'd come halfway across the world only to get stumped by Berecombe high street. Of course, they blamed us for taking all the signposts down, but they had maps.' Ruby's indignation came across loud and clear even after seventy-five years.

'Anyways, I was still standing there, mouth open, looking gormless, when this one soldier leaps out of the jeep nearest me and runs up to me. I didn't know whether to run away or kiss him.' She sniggered. 'If I'd had half a brain, I'd have kissed him then and there. On the lips an' all. Oh, Ashley, he was a looker. Golden-brown hair, all shiny it was, and the greenest eyes I've ever seen on a body. And he had a dimple in his cheek you could drown in. I thought I'd died and met Gary Cooper. Well, he picked me up, swung me around, gave me a right old smacker on the cheek and said, "This is for you, little lady," and gave me the biggest bar of chocolate I'd ever seen in my life. Chocolate, can you imagine? Even before the rationing it was a once-a-week treat, and even then I'd only be allowed a little bar of Fry's.'

Ashley smiled. 'What happened then?'

'Then he got hauled back into his jeep and they all went off up the hill, belching fumes and scattering dust. I think I stood there for a full five minutes staring at that bar of chocolate.'

'What happened to it?'

'Oh, it was delicious. I shared it out. We had one bitty piece a day, Florrie, Jimmy and me, until it had all gone. Never had anything that tasted as good. The sugar! Went right to my head and I swear it dissolved my teeth, it were that sweet.'

'Oh, so Jimmy was around by that point?'

'Yes, he'd come back from the hospitals. They'd done all they could for him.' Ruby shuddered. 'But that scar. It was a right nasty one. Hard to hide and he was very self-conscious about it. Tried to make the best of it but he preferred to keep to the back of the shop doing the paperwork, leaving me and Florrie to serve. Mind you, I think the real problem was the scars you couldn't see, the ones inside. I used to come to at night to hear him screaming the place down. Something about the sea being on fire. Florrie used to have to get the doctor sometimes. Cost her a fortune.'

'Poor man.'

Ruby sucked her teeth in agreement and fell silent.

'But you were friends?' Ashley asked. 'With Jimmy, I mean.' Somehow she sensed Ruby was holding back.

The old woman gave her a moist-eyed look. 'I was always his friend,' she said. 'Despite everything. It's just that Chet complicated things.' She sniffed and dabbed her eyes with her handkerchief. 'It's all such a long time ago now, but I regret what I did. I'll regret it to my dying day. Young Petra sang "We'll Meet Again", but we never did, Jimmy and me – meet again, I mean. So the least I could do was say goodbye at his passing. That's why I came to the funeral, see. To say sorry to Jimmy. To say sorry for breaking his heart.'

Serena chose that moment to bustle back into the square. Striding up to them, she stood, hands on hips. 'Oh Mother, you haven't been going on about the war again? You know how much it upsets you.' She pointed a belligerent finger at Ashley. 'I've just about had enough of this. Leave my mother alone. Can't you see how distressed all your questions make her? It's time we went home. And I mean London!'

'Oh no, you can't leave now,' Ashley blurted out. She'd become fond of the old woman. Besides, she was desperate to know the rest of the story; she was sure there was more.

'I think you'll find we can,' Serena bit out. She lifted her mother up by the arm, none too gently.

'No, I'm not ready to go yet.' Ruby held onto the trestle table for support. 'You can, our Serena. I've a mind to stay a while longer.'

'Oh honestly, Mother, how on earth are you going to manage that? I have to get back, as well you know. And you're coming with me.'

'As a matter of fact I've been invited to stay with someone. Here, in Berecombe.'

'Who with?' Serena stared at her mother. 'Oh, not that awful Biddy woman? You know the rumours are that she made all of her money running a brothel, don't you? Not only that, she now writes smutty books! As if I'd let you stay with anyone like that. You're coming back to London this minute, so stop arguing.' She collected the old woman's things and marched her off, holding her around the shoulders, half carrying her along.

Biddy, still resplendent in her green suit and enormous hat, arrived then, Elvis scampering along behind. 'Oh, was that Ruby and Serena leaving? I was just about to explain where the bungalow is.'

'She was coming to stay with you, I understand?' Ashley said, still reeling from the revelation that Biddy had been a madam and was now an author of erotica.

'Arthur and I are delighted to have her. I know Serena has to get back to work and Ruby wanted to stay in town for a few more days. We were going to give her the guest suite. It's just been done out.'

'I don't think she'll be coming to you, Biddy,' Ashley said. 'I think she's just been kidnapped by her own daughter. The only place she's heading is back home to London.'

For the first and possibly last time, Biddy was rendered speechless.

## Chapter Twenty-Eight

It was an evening in late April and the main bar area of The Henville was looking magnificent. The black-tie event, anticipated for weeks, couldn't have a better setting. One wall was dominated by mullioned windows against which shelves had been built on which a shimmering arrangement of blue and cut glass sparkling in the light. On the glossy wood bar were huge bowls of limes and lemons, citrussy bright against ice and ready to be added to the cocktails which were being served, along with champagne. Waiters in blue and gold livery passed through the crowds holding aloft platters full of tiny canapés.

Ashley snaffled one. Popping an innocuous-looking biscuit into her mouth, she practically swooned as the flavour exploded on her tongue. 'You have got to try one of those,' she said to Petra who was standing next to her. 'Something parmesan-y but with...' She frowned, trying to decide what the actual flavour was. 'Oh, I don't know, but it's wonderful.'

'Amateur,' Petra admonished. Taking one for herself, she bit into it, chewed thoughtfully then announced, 'Gruyere with cayenne pepper, buttery and as light as a feather. And you're right, wonderful.'

They accepted a flute of champagne from the astonishingly good-looking waiter who offered. Ashley eyed him with interest and, once he'd moved on, whispered, 'Do you think they only employ drop-dead gorgeous staff here?'

Petra giggled. 'Wouldn't you, given half a chance?'

'I don't know. Isn't it discriminatory or something?'

'Probably, but I bet it boosts the profits! By the way, you're looking gorg tonight. That silver-grey looks great with your colouring.'

'Thanks.' Ashley smoothed down the silk. 'I liked these ruffles,' she said, tweaking the frills that ran from each shoulder to her waist. 'But I wasn't too sure about the back.'

Petra took her by the shoulder and turned her around. She gave a low whistle. 'You're joking, aren't you? That's what makes it so fabby. All demure and prim at the front, but you're practically naked at the back.

How do these straps work?' She lifted a ruffle-covered one. 'Oh I see, they run right under your armpit, so it leaves your back bare until the waist. Sexy!'

'Not sure about that!' Ashley giggled. 'The leather seats in Noah's car gave me a shock when I sat back! Still, you can't say it's not warm and toasty in here.' Ashley glanced over at the enormous fire roaring in the inglenook. She fanned herself. 'I'm boiling.'

'Suppose that's the trouble with April, you never know what the weather's going to be like. Just have another drink and you won't notice. Or try a mojito – they've got ice in.'

Ashley surveyed Petra over her glass. They were becoming good friends. 'And talking about dresses, that jungle-print material is amazing.'

'It's good, isn't it?' Petra swished her full skirts. 'Vintage from a little place I know in Bridport. I'm particularly fond of the toucans. And the Jenny WRENs are performing later, so I needed something with impact.' She paused. 'So we're all gussied up, as Tess would say, but not an unattached man to be seen.' She looked around the crowded room which was humming with conversation against a background sound of a pianist playing a baby grand. 'It's true,' she added, as Ashley laughed. 'There's Ken and Tess over there, talking to Millie. That gorgeous blond man in the divine suit is her husband Jed. The curvy woman in the white Marilyn Monroe dress is Amy from the bookshop, whom I think you've met, and the tousle-haired man with the wicked blue eyes is Patrick Carroll, her boyfriend, who just happens to be the writer. Yes,' she emphasized, at Ashley's rounded eyes. '*The* writer. Eleri is the sylph-like creature dressed in sea-green and blue chiffon hanging off Alex, who owns the hotel; they're completely loved-up and run this place together. Alex is Jed's older brother – you can see the resemblance.' She blew out a breath. 'Everyone else seems to be in a couple too. Oh and look, Beryl's here with her husband; they're standing by the piano singing along with the show tunes.'

'It gets worse – even Biddy's got her man,' Ashley added mournfully. 'That's her Arthur over there. Looks like it's you and me tonight.'

'Don't get me wrong, girl, I mean, you look hot tonight,' Petra grinned, 'but I'm strictly into men.' Putting their empty glasses on a nearby table, she asked, 'So, tell me what went on with Ruby?' Fishing in her tiny clutch, she added, 'Speaking of which, this came for you at the café. Old-lady handwriting and a London postmark. I'd hazard a guess it's from her.'

'Thanks.' Taking the envelope, Ashley saw it was addressed:

*To Ashley via Petra*
*c/o Millie Vanilla's Café*
*Berecombe*
*East Devon*

'Lucky it arrived. No postcode.' Opening it, she pulled out a couple of sheets of paper covered in the same spidery handwriting and signed *Ruby*. 'It *is* from her.' Putting it safely in her own evening bag, she said, 'I'll read it later. Poor woman. Marched off by her well-meaning but humourless daughter. I'm glad she got in touch.'

'So what did happen?'

'Stand up row, in front of everyone at the tea party. I think you'd gone by that point. Turns out Serena had to get back to London. I think she's got this swanky gallery or shop or something she runs, but Ruby didn't want to budge. Serena didn't take kindly to her mother organizing to stay with Biddy and Arthur.'

'Did Biddy put her foot down?'

'Turned up too late, unfortunately. Ruby and Serena had gone. I think she was rather disappointed. Still, it was probably just as well. That she missed them, I mean.'

'Too right,' Petra said, feelingly. 'I wouldn't argue with Biddy.'

'I'm not sure I'd pick a fight with Serena either.'

Ashley pulled a face. 'So, unless there's more in the letter, it means no more Ruby stories. I didn't even get to hear about Chet.'

'Chet?'

'The GI she met. I've got a feeling she fell for him.'

'Wouldn't be surprised. All those offers of nylons and ciggies and chewing gum. Would turn any girl's head. Maybe you could ring her?'

'She lives with Serena. Doubt I'd get past her. I'm just cross with myself for not recording what she said at the tea party. It was wonderful stuff about how she met Chet for the first time and how she broke Jimmy's heart. I'm assuming Jimmy was in love with her but she was in love with Chet.' The letter in her handbag silently begged to be read but it seemed rude to do so at a party. Besides, she'd rather keep it to savour later, especially if it contained more details about Chet. 'Noah's not very happy with me.'

'Where is Noah, anyway?'

'Oh, he'll be schmoozing someone. He's always on the cadge for funding for the museum.'

'He's done great with all this.' Petra grabbed a couple more glasses of champagne, handed one to Ashley and used her own flute to point at the glamorous room.

'He's a star at this sort of thing,' Ashley said loyally. 'He's not one to be argued with either.' She giggled again, the bubbles having gone to her head. 'He's even persuaded Mike Love, the theatre director, and his wife, to do the promises auction later. And you know who his wife is, don't you? Only Theodora Bart, the actress.'

'Oh, I love her!' Petra exclaimed. Then she pulled a sympathetic face. 'No Eddie?'

Ashley shrugged, her mood dipping swiftly. 'Haven't heard from him. He said he'd try to get back in time for this, but it doesn't look like he has.'

'Oh well,' Petra put her hand through Ashley's arm. 'As many cocktails as we can get down our necks, fine dining, dancing later – it's going to be hell, but we'll just have to try our hardest to have a good time somehow.' She began to move them to the dining room, adding, 'And if we have no choice, we can fight over Sean Tizzard. He's the only other single man I know!'

## Chapter Twenty-Nine

By the time she'd ploughed through crab with lime and coconut, salmon en croute, a sinful chocolate cup and most of a bottle of prosecco, Ashley was basking in the warm glow of having eaten good food and drunk fine wine. She tried to ignore the empty place at their table, which had presumably been Eddie's, and chatted to Beryl instead. It was just as well she was surprisingly good company. On Ashley's other side, Noah was wrapped up in conversation with Petra.

The auction of promises was run with immaculate efficiency by Theodora Bart – who called everyone darling – and her husband, Mike. A great whooping went up when Beryl narrowly outbid a competitive Biddy to win Sean Tizzard, who had very sportingly offered to do whatever was required of him for a day.

Their table also struck lucky when Petra won big on the raffle and scooped up a five-course tasting menu meal for two. On her way back from collecting her prize, Petra leaned over Ashley and whispered, 'I wonder whom I should take?'

'Me, obviously, but only if my cousin is busy.' Ashley grinned back. 'How was it, shaking hands with a superstar?'

'Aw, she was so nice. So normal, if you know what I mean. And don't you just love that dress she's got on? That deep-green velvet looks so good with her colouring. Proper Hollywood, she looks.' Petra looked up at the stage where Theodora and Mike had been replaced by the mayor, Alex Henville, and Noah. 'Ooh, speeches now. Best get myself off, neck some coffee and try to sober myself up, ready for our performance.' She walked off, only a little wobbly on her high heels.

Ashley watched her departure with fondness. Petra was someone she was glad to have in her life. Good fun, uncomplicated and talented. She was looking forward to hearing the Jenny WRENs sing later.

Beryl nudged her and offered more wine. 'We might need a top-up if the speeches go on. I'm sure your Noah will keep it brief, but the mayor loves an opportunity to let rip.' She tutted, her dangly diamante earrings glinting. 'He was always the same, even back at school.

232

Liked the sound of his own voice.' She poured out the remainder of the prosecco for them both.

'Thanks, Beryl.' They clinked glasses. 'And may I say how stylish you look tonight.' It was true. Beryl's silver pixie-cut was complemented by a shimmery pale-pink tunic over narrow black trousers and spike-heeled boots.

'Well thank you, my lovely. What a nice thing to say. I do like an excuse to dress up. It's good to put on the glad rags, isn't it? Just wish I could do it more often.'

'It is.' Ashley thought for a minute, the mayor's voice droning on and fading into the background. 'You know,' she began slowly, an image of Petra in her sexy uniform forming. 'What we need is another opportunity to dress up, and I know just the thing – a 40s-inspired dance!'

'Oh Ashley, that's a splendid idea,' Beryl said. She glanced over to the table of US veterans who were appearing to doze off. 'I thought at the time that a formal black-tie event like this wasn't quite the ticket. I don't think any of our guests will last the pace beyond coffee. But I suppose tonight is more about fundraising, and quite right too.'

'Perhaps we should make it a tea dance, then?'

'And hold it in the afternoon!'

'At Millie's!'

'At Millie's,' Beryl echoed. 'Do you know, I think they might have had something similar there before.'

'But not a 40s-themed one?'

'No, dear. It was back when poor Millie was trying to keep the café afloat. We had another café which opened briefly and it hit Millie's trade rather hard. The Blue Elephant's closed now, thank goodness. Their coffee was cheaper but it wasn't nearly as nice as Millie's. There it's always made with love, I think.'

Ashley regarded Beryl fondly. She was someone else she was glad to have in her life. Beryl was, there was no other word for it, *nice*. 'Well, I'll put it to Noah and see what he says. I think he said something about a steam train ride and picnic for VE Day, so we'll have to make sure it doesn't clash with that. Let's hope our guests can stay on for a while.'

'I think two are going back to America quite soon but the others, I believe, are staying much longer.'

'Good. That gives me time to get it organized.'

'It'll be a lot of work though, my lovely.'

'It will.' Ashley looked around the room. Biddy was fussing over Elvis, completely failing to hide her boredom. The little poodle, dressed in a sparkly tangerine bowtie to match his owner's outfit, was being fed titbits of salmon. Andrea from Fir Trees Hall wiggled her fingers in a subtle wave. Erica, sitting on the same table, smiled. Ken and Tess Tizzard looked to be drinking their way through the speeches, but Tess caught her glance, rolled her eyes and tapped her watch meaningfully, which made Ashley giggle. And, in the far corner of the room, Keeley and Chloe had their heads close together, having a whispered conversation, a recorder on the table in front of them. Ashley couldn't believe that, in a few short weeks, she had so many new people in her life, that she'd made so many friends. She smiled warmly at Beryl. And such a wide variety of people. She looked at Biddy again, who was now straightening the poodle's bowtie. Who would have thought she'd be good friends with an ex-madam and erotic author! She let a giggle escape.

'But you've got the hang of Berecombe now, haven't you?' Beryl continued. 'You know we'll come together to help you out.'

Ashley took her hand, too emotional to say anything.

They were interrupted by Ken Tizzard, who slid into Noah's empty seat. 'Are you ever going to come and see me at the workshop?' he demanded.

'I'm so sorry, Ken,' Ashley whispered. 'I keep meaning to but I'm just so busy. What did you want to see me about?'

'Got a job for you. Receptionist first, but there might be a bit of teaching involved, if you're interested.'

'Oh Ken, I'd love that. Can I say a definite yes to the

receptionist's job and a maybe to the teaching? I'm still not sure if I'm up to it.'

Ken shrugged. 'Of course.' He stood up and yelled above the applause that greeted the end of the speeches. 'Have a think and let me know. No hurry,' he said before shooting back to Tess, who was now attacking his pint of beer.

'Well, isn't that marvellous. You've got an excuse to stay with us a while longer,' Beryl said. 'I'm so pleased. And, what with the tea dance and a new job, it's going to keep you extra busy.' She wiggled her eyebrows. 'And now the boring speeches are over, are you coming to dance?'

The thought of dancing made Ashley feel sick. She hadn't attempted anything like it since the accident. She watched as people drifted into the ballroom. 'I'll stay here if you don't mind, Beryl. I'm going to have another coffee and some of those petit fours.'

'Well, if you're sure you won't get lonely.'

Thinking of the letter, still unread in her bag, Ashley assured her she'd be fine. She waited until everyone from the table had left and, ignoring the staff around her quietly clearing up, she took out the letter and began to read.

## Chapter Thirty

*Hello Ashley dearie,*

*I hope this gets to you. Serena wouldn't hear of me staying in Berecombe any longer so I'm back home. Maybe it's for the best. I'm not sure I could have told you this part of the story face to face. I've grown very fond of you, Ashley, and don't want you thinking badly of me.*

*I came to Jimmy's funeral to ask for his forgiveness. Forgiveness for breaking his heart. Twice he asked me to marry him and twice I refused. The second time he wrote, I'd been back in London for a few years by then. It must have been 1950. I was working in an insurance office. Not very exciting but then nothing was back then. The war was over but we still had rationing and you still had to pick your way around the bomb craters. Grey and dust. That's all I* remember from that time. Still, I was lucky to have a job. Once the men came back from war, we all got pushed out from what we was doing.

Jimmy wrote and sent me that posh picture that was on display at the funeral, the one taken in the studio. Said he'd got a good job with the council and would I consider going back to Devon and marrying him. I turned him down. Couldn't face returning to Berecombe. Not after what had happened.

You see, in May 1944 I fell pregnant with a baby. Don't judge me, Ashley. I know I was barely sixteen but things were different then. The December before, a stray bomb landed near the mill. Killed two little girls. They was evacuees up from Plymouth. Supposed to be safe in Berecombe. Playing Pooh sticks on the river, they were. Neither above ten and regulars in the shop. It got you thinking. Alive one minute, but you could be dead the next. It made you grab what little bit of happiness you could get. I was walking out with Chet by then and one thing led to another. Of course, he went off that June, leaving me with a bun in the oven.

Florrie found out and told Jimmy, and they promised to look after me. And they did. Except, when the news got to Berecombe, we heard most of the boys who went to Omaha wouldn't be coming back. Wouldn't be going anywhere ever again. And that included Chet. Jimmy told me. Ever so gentle, he was. Sat me down on the settee in the front room and held my hand. Held me when I cried too. We sat up all the long night, talking and crying, and he promised to make things right. He offered to marry me so I'd be respectable.

I tried loving Jimmy, I really did, but I couldn't, not as he wanted me to. I lived with the Larcombes for a bit longer but I couldn't bear being in the town. Too many memories of Chet, you see. I told Jimmy I couldn't marry him and left for London. Told him I wanted to do my bit. Broke his heart but I didn't know what I was doing. My heart was broken too.

So there you have it. One day I'll write and maybe tell you of the larks me and Chet got up to, the dances and the fun. Even though there was a war on, we still had fun. Even though we hadn't known each other long, it was as if we'd always known each other. He was the love of my life, Ashley. I wouldn't have gone with him if he wasn't.

Maybe one day I'll be back in Berecombe. I'd love to have more chats with you, Ashley dearie. Although it's brought up some painful memories, it was good to remember those days too. In the words of dear old Vera, I hope 'We'll Meet Again'!

Fondest Regards,

Ruby

Ashley sat back, her hands shaking slightly, her head reeling. Poor Ruby. And welcome though the letter was, there was so much that was still missing. How had it gone from Chet giving Ruby a bar of chocolate to them going out? How had Jimmy felt about it? Back from the war and scarred, only to lose the girl he loved to a GI? She remembered Biddy saying she thought he'd had his heart broken and he'd never married. So it was Ruby who had broken it.

She sat up in frustration. What had happened to the baby? It couldn't have been Serena – she was too young. What had happened to Ruby when she went back to London? Scanning the letter top, she was relieved to see an address in Blackheath. At least she could write back. And she needed to – she had so many questions.

'Well, it's a good thing I'm staying in Berecombe for now. Means I can see what more I can find out,' she murmured.

'Can I say how delighted I am that you're staying in town a little while longer,' a voice behind her said.

Ashley swivelled round in her seat. 'Eddie,' she cried in delight. 'You came!'

## Chapter Thirty-One

He led her into the evening air onto a long terrace which ran the length of the dining room. It was open on one side to the April night. Music carried from the ballroom, a muted whisper of sound, but perfect. The only illumination came from the white lights which were thronged along the wall. In the distant countryside the darkness fell lightly like the softest of cashmere and blanketed them in solitude. The cold didn't touch Ashley; her heart was too fired up with looking at the man in front of her. Like most of the other male guests, he was in a dinner suit. His preferred clothes choice was casual but, when he dressed up, like tonight or for Jimmy's funeral, the effect was devastating. He'd had his hair cut and the sharp jawline revealed was accentuated by the crisp white collar of his dress shirt. Some men wore a bowtie with a shade of embarrassment but, on Eddie, it just looked right.

'You look perfect,' she breathed.

He gave a throaty laugh. 'You don't look too bad yourself. Guess we both scrub up well.'

'I'm so pleased you're back.'

'You know what? So am I. There's just something drawing me back to this town.' His eyes gleamed. 'Just don't know what it is.'

'How's your mum?'

'She's good. Had a relapse, but doing better now.'

'I'm glad.'

'I would have come back sooner but,' he paused, 'I had some stuff to sort out.'

'Oh.'

They went to sit on a white bench which ran under the lights. He didn't elaborate, so Ashley filled him in on the parade and the tea party, finishing by telling him about the letter. 'So Ruby had an affair with Chet the GI. He was the love of her life but he died on D-Day.'

Eddie whistled. 'So we got it wrong. She doesn't hate all things American.'

'Quite the contrary. She had his baby.' She felt him stiffen.

'Jeez.'

'You know, I always wondered if Chet and your

242

grandfather were the same man. It was something about how Ruby reacted to you the first time she saw you. As if she'd seen a ghost.'

Eddie laughed ruefully. 'Guess he can't be, not if Chet died at Omaha. My grandfather definitely survived the war. My mom and I are proof of that.'

'Maybe it was just the American accent. Maybe that and being in Berecombe triggered a memory.'

'Maybe. I haven't got very far with my grandaddy's story, have I?'

'There's time. You said you had some stuff to sort out at home?'

'Yeah.' Eddie pulled a face. 'Things got kind of complicated.'

She reached out and touched him. This wasn't the reunion she'd dreamed of. He seemed distant, wary, but she couldn't resist taking his hand.

He twisted to her. 'Ash, I've got something to tell you.'

He got no further, as Ashley drew him to her and kissed him. She heard him groan as he slid an arm around her waist and his hand found the skin of her naked back. His touch seared heat where the cold night air struck. The kiss deepened and his other hand found her breast and caressed it through the slippery silk, making her nipple proud. She reached up and cupped his neck, pulling him in deeper.

And then he froze. Backing off, he took her hands from around his neck. The cold sank into the space between them, creating a gulf she feared was unnavigable. She could see lust glazing his hazel eyes, but there was something else there too. Guilt?

Ashley's heart flipped. 'What have you to tell me, Eddie?'

He turned away from her slightly. 'Before I start, firstly I want to make clear I didn't see this situation coming. Any of it. And secondly, I don't want to just be friends with you, Ashley. I knew that from the very first moment I saw you.'

'Go on.' It came out on a cracked whisper.

He looked down and scuffed one shiny dress shoe against the other, leaving a trail of dust. 'Remember I told you about Bree and how she broke my heart?'

She nodded. A sense of foreboding stole over her.

He grimaced and rubbed his chest as if in pain. 'She messed with my head. Whenever I went out with someone else, she'd reel me right back in and then spit me right back out again.' He glanced at her quickly. 'I'm not proud of being so manipulated, but when you're in the middle of something it's hard to back out. I just went along with her, wherever that meant.'

Ashley nodded, thinking of all the times she'd just

gone along with Piers. Surfing, mountain climbing, when she had little interest in either. It wasn't quite the same but it gave her some understanding.

'It's extra complicated, as she's good friends with Mom. Mom hoped Bree would settle down sometime – and with me – and I suppose I hoped the same.'

'What happened?'

'I got the job offer over here. It seemed a great opportunity.'

'So you gave Bree an ultimatum?'

Eddie winced. 'I didn't, but she misread it as such. We had a huge fight. She said it was all over for good, stormed out before we could talk things over, and I left on the next flight. We tried to talk it through again when I went back at Christmas and,' he hesitated, 'there was a sort of reconciliation, but I knew in my gut, for me anyway, it was over by then. I didn't want her to hurt me again. Coming to England had given me the head space I needed. I could see there was no future for us. It was hard, though. I've known her since I was a freshman in high school. She's been in my life for a long time.'

'Did you see her when you went back home this time?'

'I had to. I wanted to see Bowie. I'll never get over having to leave him, but it wasn't fair to uproot him.' His mouth tightened. 'Turns out Bree had to have him put down. Happened the day before I got back, so I never got to say goodbye to the old fella. He'd become really sick since Christmas and she was torn up about having to make the decision. She had some news for me too.'

Ashley gasped and covered his hand with hers. 'I'm so sorry, Eddie. That's awful. For you and her.'

'Yeah. I'd had him since he was a puppy. He was the cutest black Lab pup you've ever seen.' He glanced at Ashley and she could see tears in his eyes. 'I'll never know if I did the right thing, leaving him at home. Bree had taken him in for a check-up and the vet said he was in a huge amount of pain. She had to make the decision straight away. It was really hard on her.' He tightened his grip on her hand and sucked in a harsh breath, then continued. 'I needed to see her to say thank you for doing that. It's never an easy decision, even though you know you're doing the right thing. I also had to tell her about you. About how I'm developing feelings for you. I am, you know. I knew that early on. But I had to talk things over with Bree. I owed her that, at least.'

Ashley remained silent.

'We met up. She came to visit Mom. We talked. I told her about you.'

'Oh.'

'And she gave me her blessing. Told me you sounded perfect. Gave me the closure I was looking for, I guess.'

Ashley didn't understand him needing Bree's blessing but she could see it meant a great deal to him. The closure she understood a little more. She and Piers had never ended their relationship as such – it had simply fizzled out. Perhaps she could learn from Eddie. Face things head on.

'I needed that,' Eddie continued, 'before I came to find you and tell you I think I'm falling in love with you.'

'Oh.' She was aware she was repeating herself but couldn't help it.

He kissed her, gently this time. Taking his jacket off, he draped it around her bare shoulders. 'Don't want you getting cold. There's something else I need to explain and it might take a while.'

'Eddie?' A woman's voice sounded, cutting the atmosphere like a knife. 'Are you out here, buddy?' She strode into view. She was tall and dressed in a chic black cocktail dress. 'Oh there you are, honey,' she added, in a distinct east coast American accent.

She could be only one person.

Bree marched up to them. 'Why are you sitting out here in the cold? Come on in, the band's great.' She held out a hand, which Ashley shook numbly. 'And you must be the Ashley I've heard so much about. It's so great to meet you. Come back in, both of you, it's freezing out here.' Caressing an almost indistinguishable bump under

247

the black velvet of her dress, she added on a giggle, 'And I'm dying for more of that champagne but,' she fluttered her lashes coquettishly, 'in my condition I really shouldn't!'

## Chapter Thirty-Two

As Ashley stared at her, Bree backed away, her fingers to her mouth. 'Oh boy, I can see he hasn't told you. My bad.' Her voice was contrite but a hard glitter in her eyes suggested something else. 'I'll go find a drink and some food.' She rolled her eyes at Ashley as if seeking feminine solidarity. 'Now the morning sickness is over, I'm permanently starved! Hope they've got something left; we arrived too late for dinner.' Glancing between her and Eddie, Bree pulled a face and tiptoed out in an overly dramatic and comical fashion.

Ashley stared at Eddie, her mouth hanging open. So much had happened in the last few minutes, she had difficulty focusing. 'Bree's here? And *pregnant?*'

Petra's voice drifted through, sweet and clear. The

Jenny WRENs' set must have begun. She was singing 'We'll Meet Again'. Ruby and Chet's reunion had never happened. Chet had never returned from war. Now, another drama involving an American and a baby was playing out. The parallels were almost comical. But Ashley was in no mood to laugh. She'd longed for Eddie's return with every fibre of her being, but he didn't seem to have any idea how much this news had hurt. Through the fog of shock she was aware he'd taken her hand and was speaking.

'Bree told me she was pregnant when I saw her last week. She's about four months, so it dates from—'

'Your sort of reconciliation at Christmas. Yes, thank you, Eddie, I can do the maths. It *is* your baby, then.' She snatched her hand out of his and crossed her arms. She was beginning to shake but couldn't tell if it was from cold or shock.

'Pretty sure it is.'

'You're *pretty* sure?'

'Bree's told me it's my baby, so I believe her. I want to be involved, of course, but I can assure you Bree and I are over.'

'How can it be over when she's having your baby? And what's she even doing here anyway?' Ashley's brain refused to work properly. Whatever reunion she'd envisaged on Eddie's return, it wasn't this.

'She decided to come over to see where I'm teaching. Wanted to travel while she could.'

'How nice.' Ashley didn't bother to hide the sarcasm. 'And is she staying with you?'

Eddie gave a short laugh. 'Bree likes her luxury too much to stay in my one-bed in Southernhay. She's in a hotel. Ashley, I can't tell you how sorry I am about all this.'

'It's a shame you didn't think about being sorry when you were sleeping with Bree!' she bit out. 'Didn't you use contraception?'

Eddie hung his head. 'Okay, I deserved that. Yeah, but nothing's one hundred percent safe.' He met her gaze. 'Trust me, it's not how I saw the beginning of our relationship playing out, but you can see, can't you, that I can't abandon the baby?'

'I can't see how we can have a relationship, Eddie. Not now.'

'Ashley, be fair, I hadn't met you at Christmas. Do you honestly think I would've slept with Bree if I had? Don't you know me at all?'

'That's the problem, Eddie. We hardly know one another. You know nothing about me, and I now realize I know less than nothing about you.'

'I know I want to get to know you, Ashley. Maybe build something with you.'

'But I'm not sure *I* can, knowing you're having a baby with another woman. You must see that.'

'It's the shock. It took me some time to figure it all out. But I'm coming round to seeing it as one of my best friends having a baby. It just happens to be *my* baby. I've always wanted children, Ashley.'

The thought speared pain into her very being. 'Eddie, all we've done is kiss. If you'd asked me before you went home, I would've said we were friends.'

'More than friends, Ashley. You must know I want to be more than friends.'

She waved ineffectually at the night, at the romantic white lights and the mist hanging on the hills, dark in the distance. 'I don't know what to think. You've never made your feelings clear.'

'I thought I had. With every kiss.'

'And there was Bree in the background.'

'I tried telling you about her, I really did. It's just not that easy to unpick it all. There never seemed the right time to tell you.' He ran an exasperated hand through his hair, anger beginning to bite. 'Jeez. Every time I tried, we got interrupted. She was a big part of my life for so long. She hurt me. I left. I met you.'

'And now there's a baby.' Ashley remembered Petra saying men rarely came without baggage. An on-off ex-girlfriend she could've coped with, but this... She wondered what Petra would do? But Petra was a different woman. Ashley had fought long and hard to get to this point in her life. She wasn't sure another woman's baby had a place in it.

'Ash, I'm struggling here. I can't change what's happened, what happened before I even met you. I've tried to be as honest as I can. I'm thirty-six years old. I've got a history; you must have expected that. What do you want? The fairy-tale?'

'Yes. No. I don't know.' The confusion in her head worsened. 'Of course you have a relationship history. I do too. But you're having a baby with your ex. It'll never be history, will it? Bree will always be in your life from now on because she's having your child.'

Ashley stood up, feeling sick. She handed him back his jacket, trying not to look at his stricken face. Was she was about to throw away the best thing that had ever happened to her? 'I don't know, Eddie. I really don't know.' She shook off his attempt to take her hand again and added, suddenly decisive, 'No, I *do* know. I can't cope with this. I'll try to be your friend but there's no future for any other kind of relationship between us. None at all. Not now. Maybe not ever.'

And then she walked away, stumbling a little and refusing to look back.

Bree found Eddie where Ashley had left him. His hands were dangling listlessly between his knees, his head down. A picture of abject misery.

'You didn't come back in, honey,' she purred. 'I've been waiting for an age back there. The little girlfriend gone?' She sat down next to him, captured his hand and pressed it to her velvet-covered breasts. 'If you don't mind my saying, she seemed whiney, if not a little hysterical.'

He turned on her. 'Don't you dare say that.' Snatching his hand away, he pointed a furious finger. 'Don't ever say that about her. She's honest and true and brave, and has more goodness in her little finger than you have in your entire body.'

Bree backed off, holding up her hands in surrender. Changing tack, she said, 'Okay, big boy. What's eating you?'

'You know damn well what. You couldn't let me tell her, could you?'

She pulled a mock-innocent face. 'Tell her what, baby?'

'Aw, jeez Bree. Will you ever change? Will you ever stop playing games? You knew I wanted to tell Ashley myself. Break it to her in some way she might understand. But no, you had to come wading in, be the drama queen. As per usual.'

'You used to like me being a drama queen, Ed.' She pouted at him suggestively.

He gave a short, harsh laugh. 'If the scales hadn't already dropped from my eyes, then they sure have now.' He shook his head, wonderingly. 'What did I ever see in you, Bree? Why did I let you play me for all those years?' He surged to his feet.

Bree hung onto his arm. 'She'll come round. Just a big shock, is all.'

'Oh, she'll come round because I'll make damn sure she does.' He shook her off. 'I don't care how long it takes, I'm going to do everything I can to help her understand. What *you're* incapable of understanding, Bree, is I love this girl. I love her in a way I've never loved anyone else. Certainly not you.'

She blanched.

'Until I met Ashley I didn't realize how love could make me feel. I hadn't realized how happy I could be. And I was never happy with you, Bree. Never! You'll have my support with the baby, I'll raise the kid, I'll be there for my child, but that's all *you* get.' He went to go and then changed his mind. 'And one more thing. I'd advise, very seriously, that you don't do anything, I repeat, *anything* to upset Ashley. She's going to be co-parenting with me. She's going to be around. I don't care what I have to do, but she's going to be there. Ashley's going to be in my life!'

## Chapter Thirty-Three

Ashley huddled on the sofa in the little flat and stared glassily at a blank television. It was three in the morning, but she was too cold and miserable to move.

'Oh good, you're still up,' Noah said, as he poked his head around the door. 'Fancy a cuppa and a debrief? I'm too wired to sleep.' Then he saw her properly and dropped to his knees at her side. 'Ash, what's wrong?' he asked, aghast. He took her hands in his. 'You're frozen.' Chafing them between his, he added, 'I'll make tea and you can tell me all about it.'

As he clattered about in the kitchen, he told her about the ball, about how successful it had been, about how much money had been raised, about how much the American veterans had enjoyed it. Ashley let his chatter slide over her head, only partly processing what he was saying. Sitting up, she accepted the throw he tucked around her shoulders.

'No wonder you're cold, there's nothing to that dress,' he scolded and pressed her fingers around a mug of tea.

Ashley mustered a smile. 'You sound like my mother.'

'Well, I suppose I am *in loco parentis*.' He winced. 'But that makes me sound ancient. Spill the beans then, coz. What's happened?'

She looked at him, eyes huge with misery and confusion. 'Truth?'

'Truth. As ever. Nothing less.' He settled on the floor at her feet. 'Is it something to do with Eddie?'

Ashley's lips twisted. 'How did you guess?'

'I saw him with a rather chic woman dressed in black. Girlfriend?'

'Ex.'

'So what's the problem?' He drank some tea.

'She's having his baby.'

'Is she, now?' Noah let out a low whistle and put his mug down in shock. He grimaced. 'Forgive me, but I thought you and he were getting close.'

'We are. *Were*,' Ashley corrected herself bitterly.

'That's awful. He never struck me as the sort of bloke who would play women.'

'I don't think he is.' She sighed wearily. 'It's more complicated than that.'

'How can it be more complicated? You wait until the next time I see him. I'll let him know he doesn't mess with my cousin and get away with it.'

Despite herself, Ashley managed a grin. Noah's protectiveness was both touching and funny. 'It's all right, you don't need to defend my honour. It all happened at Christmas, way before he met me.'

Noah's shoulders and indignation sank back to their normal levels. 'Thank God for that.' He flicked a glance at her ashen face. 'Might make it tricky to have a relationship with him, but not impossible.'

'No, it's impossible, Noah,' she whispered and sipped her tea.

'Why?'

There was a pause. It fell heavily between them. Eventually she spoke. 'At my last consultation, the one before I came down here, there was some discussion about my ability to have children. Because of the accident, I mean.'

'Oh, Ash!'

She shrugged. 'It depends on a lot of things, the consultant said. It's not definite, I'm still not fully healed…' She let the sentence dangle.

'But?'

'If I can't have children, I'm not sure I can start a relationship with a man who's having a baby with his ex-girlfriend, even if there's an entire ocean in between them. It would be too painful knowing I might never get to have a baby of my own with him.'

He picked up his mug and swirled the tea around thoughtfully. 'And you wanted a relationship with Eddie?'

Ashley nodded. 'Think so.' She thought about the man's intelligence and humour, his kindness and generosity of spirit. How she fizzed inside whenever they kissed. She blew out a hollow breath. Oh yes, she wanted a relationship with him, all right.

Noah bit his lip, appearing to consider what to say. 'You know, it would be one way to have a family. I mean, the world is full of blended families – is that the term? – and there are lots of step-parents who do it.'

'Yeah. Maybe. I just don't think I'm a big enough person.' She recalled what Eddie had accused her of. He'd been right. 'I think I want – wanted – the fairy-tale.'

'Fairy-tales are hard to come by, love.'

'I know. Doesn't stop you wanting them, though.'

He reached for her hand again. 'Can I be really honest here?'

'Go on,' she said, warily.

'It's just that you always react to things so quickly

and jump with both feet. Usually by jumping in the opposite direction.'

'What do you mean?'

'That bloke you were seeing at uni. Didn't work out, so the next thing, as soon as you graduated, you high-tailed it back to Ludlow. Didn't get the job teaching in Florence, so you stayed in Shropshire.'

'Hang on, Noah.' She sat up, indignant. 'Steve was a complete jerk; he didn't want me to work if we got married. Can you imagine? And the international school made it clear I wasn't right for them. What exactly was I supposed to do?'

'Okay, I'll concede Steve was a jerk, but did you ever talk to him about all that? No, you just ended it. And there could have been other teaching jobs in Italy, but what did you do? Did you apply for any others? No, you went home.'

'What's your point, Noah?' Ashley said tersely.

'That if things don't work out your way, you immediately cut them right out of your life. No negotiation. No discussion to find a way through, a way of it working out. Something bad happens and, bang, on to the next thing you go. Without a backward glance.'

Ashley shifted, uncomfortable. Noah had never talked to her so critically before.

'I'm saying this because I love you and I want you to

be happy. Life's all about compromise, Ash. And, as we get older, there's sometimes more to compromise about.'

'Like Eddie?'

'Like Eddie.'

'I don't think I can compromise about Eddie and the baby, Noah,' she said in a tight voice. 'I'm scared I'll find it too painful. Too hard. That's what's behind all this. Self-preservation. Back off, will you?'

'Aren't the best things worth fighting for? Might even be worth the pain.' Registering her anger, he sighed. 'Okay. Maybe it's as well you didn't get in too deep with Eddie, then.'

Ashley didn't bother to correct him.

'You've plenty of time to meet someone else. That's if you want to,' he added hastily, as if realizing his lack of tact.

She yawned and stretched her legs. She needed to get to bed. She didn't want anyone else, only Eddie.

'You are going to stay in Berecombe, though?' Noah looked suddenly stricken. 'You're not going to cut and run this time? I can't do this commemoration year without you, coz!' He tried for humour. 'I mean, who will do my filing?'

Ashley straightened her shoulders. She gazed at him. What would *she* do without *him*? She looked around at her little flat. Her post-accident independence had been so hard won; she didn't want to give it up now. She certainly didn't want to prove him right by running home to Ludlow and to the well-meaning but suffocating care of her parents. Eddie aside, Berecombe suited her. She felt safe here.

'Well, I have my painting,' she began slowly. 'I've only just begun getting back into that and I'd like to do more, experiment with some different styles, maybe.' She thought of Petra and Millie, of Beryl, Ken and Tess, and even Biddy. 'I've made friends here,' she added. Then she remembered Ken's offer. She slid to the edge of the sofa, positivity blunting some of the sharpness of her anger with Noah. 'And I haven't told you, have I? Ken's offered me a job. At the Arts Centre. Oh Noah, I really love this town. It's entwined itself around my heart. I don't want to leave!'

'And neither should you.' He grinned. 'You've got the memories project too, don't forget. You'll want to see that through with Ruby?'

'If I can. Might have to be by letter or phone, though. I'm not sure when she'll be back in Berecombe.'

'By whatever means is fine by me. There'll be others to interview too. You're just getting started with it all.' He clasped her fingers tightly. 'Stay, Ashley. You're putting roots down here, I can tell. And it's a good place to do that. We can find you another man, if you want one. Or woman.' He pulled a face and added cheerfully, 'Or neither. You'll be fine on your own. And you've always got your big, brave cousin to fight your corner.'

She smiled at him. Through her exhaustion, buoyed by his love and support, surged a sudden optimism. She could do this. Eddie McQueen or no Eddie McQueen. She could do this. 'And I've always got my big, brave cousin.'

'Stay, Ashley,' he implored.

'I just might.'

'And might there be a chance you could make it up with Eddie? He's too good a man to let go, Ash. He's so right for you. You must realize that.'

'I'll think about it.' She darted a quick smile, his earlier criticism still stinging. Was there a chance for a relationship with Eddie? 'Maybe, when I've had time to think it through,' she said cautiously. 'I might get used to the idea.'

'Baby steps, coz. He'll be worth it in the end.'

Ashley stared into space, an image of Eddie's warm smile filling her vision. Did she have enough strength for the fight?

Noah read her thoughts. 'Look at what you've fought these past couple of years. You've learned to walk again, battled the pain. Started a new life in a new town. Got yourself a brand-new job. Why not fight to get yourself the man you want?'

She took his hand; her cousin was telling the truth. Stating the obvious. Eddie was the man she wanted. He was the one she *needed*.

'Then, let battle commence,' she whispered, her eyes sparkling with unshed tears. 'It might take me a while but, Eddie McQueen, get ready. I'm coming for you!'

## Acknowledgments

I needed a lot of help to write this one! I hope I've
included everyone this time.

My sincere thanks go to the very lovely and talented
Colin Simmonds who furnished me with details of a
painter's life, and to Dr Pinky Jain and Dr Linzi McKerr
of Worcester University for information on academia. My
grateful thanks go to Julia Roebuck who opened up the
world of Morris Dancing, Wendy Jones who, as always,
gave medical information, and Leah Larson and Greg
Poulos for help on all things USA. Janice Rosser and the
Helen Vereker Singers helped with what it means to be in
a community choir and Janice Preston provided
information about art classes. Thank you all! I'm also
grateful that writing this book meant I had an excuse to
discuss my mother's childhood wartime memories with

her. She also helped with the titles. Thanks mum! I'm so grateful these people gave up their precious time to share their expertise; any mistakes are very much all mine.

Charlotte Ledger and her team at One More Chapter helped shape this book with brilliant editing and I am eternally grateful for their enthusiasm and expertise.

And finally, a huge thank you to you, the reader, for buying, borrowing, reading, reviewing, and supporting my books. If one thing the past two years have proved, it's that reading and books are more important than ever.

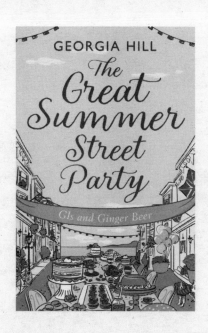

**Return to Berecombe and find out what happens next in *GIs and Ginger Beer*, the second book in the Great Summer Street Party series!**

With summer having arrived in Berecombe with sunshiny gusto, and the D-Day anniversary celebrations on the horizon, there's much to keep Ashley Lydden busy as she settles further into her new life by the seaside.

So why can't she stop thinking about Eddie McQueen?

**And don't miss *Blue Skies and Blackberry Pies*, the
third book in the Great Summer Street Party series!**

Berecombe's year of commemoration may be coming to a
close ... but the rest of Ashley Lydden's new life has only
just begun! Ashley couldn't have predicted that she'd
find herself a whole new – much happier – life in the
quiet seaside town of Berecombe, but now she can't
imagine being anywhere else.

She knows better than most though that life has a way of
surprising you when you least expect it...

## ONE MORE CHAPTER

One More Chapter is an
award-winning global
division of HarperCollins.

Sign up to our newsletter to get our
latest eBook deals and stay up to date
with our weekly Book Club!
<u>Subscribe here.</u>

Meet the team at
<u>www.onemorechapter.com</u>

Follow us!
 @OneMoreChapter_
 @OneMoreChapter
 @onemorechapterhc

Do you write unputdownable fiction?
We love to hear from new voices.
Find out how to submit your novel at
<u>www.onemorechapter.com/submissions</u>